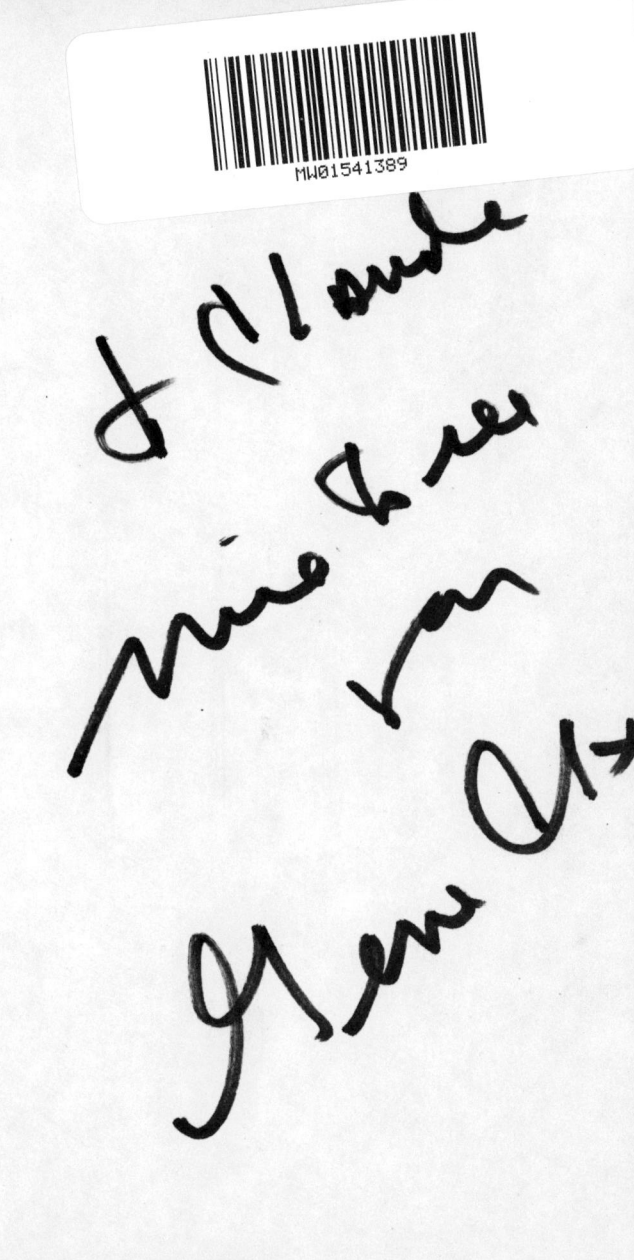

Dear Jim,

thank you
for the
card!

Love,

Other *riverrun* books by Gene Cox

GLAZED DONUTS

*PECCADILLOES
AND OTHER STRANGE ANIMALS*

The Sunset Lounge

Gene Cox

riverrun

THE SUNSET LOUNGE

A riverrun enterprises, inc. book.

This is a work of fiction, and any similarity
to any existing event, person, association or company,
whether present or past, is coincidental.

All rights reserved.
Copyright © 1997 by Gene Cox
This book may not be reproduced in whole or in part,
by mimeograph or any other means, without permission.

ISBN: 0-9649791-2-8

riverrun enterprises, inc.
Richmond, Virginia

PRINTED IN THE UNITED STATES OF AMERICA
10   9   8   7   6   5   4   3   2   1

To Ellie, with love.

*With special thanks to
Doug and Donna.*

The Sunset Lounge

JARRATT—Lenny Daniels Tisdale, Jr., a two-time killer and the last surviving member of the so-called "Poison Club" which killed several people, including two police officers, was executed last night by lethal injection.

Asked if he had a last statement, Tisdale said, "Merry Christmas." He was pronounced dead at 11:13 p.m.

Tisdale was the third man executed in Virginia this month. The execution of Dr. Roger Ragland is scheduled to take place Monday.

The Tisdale execution moves Virginia, with seven executions this year, ahead of South Carolina and Missouri for the most executions in the country for 1997. Since the resumption of the death penalty in 1982, Virginia's previous annual record was five.

—Richmond Times-Dispatch

1

Phil Jaco watched his wife carry a cup of latte into the sun room and set it on the wicker table beside him. The early winter sun peeked through the Palladian windows and warmed her face. Her blond hair glistened in its rays. Gloria was one month shy of her forty-second birthday, and a decade of sitting beside the pool nursing gin and tonics had not yet taken its toll. She could still pass, in office parlance, as a trophy wife, though she didn't act like one. Not anymore.

As Jaco watched his wife, he did not see himself. Jaco, fifty-three years old, stood a modest five feet, nine inches tall and weighed well over two hundred pounds. The navel on his protruding stomach peeked through the gap in his robe. Hairy white legs reached out below the robe and connected to feet tucked inside worn slippers. His other end wasn't much better. It featured a balding head on which Jaco would have draped a toupee, had this not been a weekend. But it was, and he didn't.

Jaco's wealth and the toupee concealed little, though he had allowed himself to imagine otherwise.

She did not look at him.

He took a sip of the coffee and winced. Not enough sugar. Damn. She reached across him and turned on the TV. The morning news show entered the room as the weekend anchor read a story about Len Tisdale's execution.

"Have you gotten the paper yet?"

Jaco grunted and shifted in his seat. The paper was his job. She did coffee, he did the paper. That was the Saturday morning division of labor, established by time and habit. To alter it would require communication, and he would rather just get the paper than become involved in a mindless conversation with his wife. He'd do it in a minute. Through the artificial Christmas tree, he watched the wind blowing leaves around in the backyard.

"Montaldo's is having a sale," she said, mostly to herself.

Grudgingly, Jaco took a sip of coffee and climbed out of his chair. Before opening the door, he pulled the sash on the robe to cover his stomach and tugged the collar tight around his neck. Not that he needed to. It was, he discovered, stepping into the sunlight, almost spring-like. A week before Christmas, and here he was actually tilting his head back to let the sun fall on him like a warm shower. He took another sip of coffee and relished the sound of the door clicking shut behind him.

The dog met him at the fence, loping up with its hair

puffed out over its eyes. Damn show dog. The dog had become unusually affectionate since its twin died, a year ago. To the dog, Jaco was the replacement. It was the best he could do. Jaco gave it a quick pat and opened the gate. As always, River Heights was silent. The houses, though not far apart, snuggled in secrecy— Leyland cypresses and mature English boxwoods helped provide a shield from each other and the outside world.

It wasn't until he got halfway down the driveway that Jaco could actually see over the boxwoods that separated him from the next-door neighbors. Not that there was anything to see besides a rather old but proud baby-blue Mercedes and a Volvo with a child's seat in the back seat. Strange, Jaco told himself: didn't know they had kids.

Without realizing it, Jaco began to whistle a tune under his breath. He composed it as he walked. At the end of the driveway, he stooped to pick up the paper. The Tisdale execution covered much of the front page. The paper had used the occasion of the execution to review the crimes that led to it, including accounts of other Richmond police officers who had died in the line of duty. But all that research was wasted on Phil Jaco. He lingered only a moment before clumsily shifting his coffee from hand to hand so he could skip to the Business section.

The main story was a fluff piece on a local businessman who said he was going to donate a portion of his Christmas sales to the United Way. Jaco shook his head and turned the page. They should have called him before running the story: he'd have given them a little dirt to spice it up. Everybody's got some dirt on them, and more often than not, Jaco could tell you what it was. Not that founding a small cookie empire hooked him directly into the underground dirt line, but he had his connections. Still, he had to admire the guy's salesmanship. Maybe next year he'd do something like that to help the holiday sales. He turned the page and held the fold open into the light.

Behind the paper, he heard soft footsteps coming down the road. The rubber patter of a jogger's shoes, he thought, glancing over the real estate stories. Then the dog growled, and the paper exploded from Jaco's hands in a crisp flash.

The first blow caught Jaco on the cheek and spun him against the mailbox. The second sent him to his knees. By the time the attacker kicked him in the stomach, Jaco was close to blacking out. Still, with the evenly timed rhythm of someone working on a punching bag in the gym, Jaco's attacker continued to work him over, and somehow, Jaco remained conscious.

"Help," he wanted to say. "Somebody help me!"

But all he could manage was a stifled gasp, as the attacker rolled him over and kicked him gruffly in the small of the back. Then, as suddenly as he had appeared, the attacker disappeared in a patter of nonchalant, jogging strides. And Jaco, lying on his back in a swath of stray newspaper sheets, listened to the high-priced stillness return to River Heights.

Now that Jaco actually needed someone—a neighbor raking the leaves, say, or a mother pushing her child in a stroller—the silence was decidedly less appealing. Only Jaco's dog stood by, sniffing curiously at the blood that ran in a crazy-veined pattern from Jaco's nose and mouth and through the cracks between the driveway's fashionable cobblestones. The dog studiously ignored Jaco himself and proved, yet again, how useless show dogs can be. Perhaps it thought of its lost mate and wondered if the substitute would also be taken away. After a moment, the dog loped back toward the house, tail curled between its legs. He didn't even retrieve the paper.

Years seemed to pass before Gloria appeared at the top of the driveway, shrieking. She'd never been exposed to violence, and now that she'd stumbled onto it at the foot of her own driveway, she found herself unable to move. For a moment, Jaco merely stared at her with the blood gurgling from his mouth.

"Damn it," he sputtered. "Do something!"

She stared uselessly at him for a moment longer and then hurried back up the driveway with the dog close behind her. Another eternity seemed to pass before Jaco heard sirens in the distance. In the wailing sound, he found hope, as he lost consciousness and leaned back against his mailbox.

Gene Cox

The sirens, however, were not for him.

2

Chandler Harris opened his refrigerator as if he expected something good to happen. A box of fuzzy mushrooms smiled at him. They had come courtesy of a brief girlfriend who, two weeks earlier, smiled hopefully as she prepared her version of Italian cuisine, then left. The relationship was such that she did not return to claim her mushrooms. Of her visit, only his memories remained, and the mushrooms. He valued neither. There was also a half-cup of milk, a full bottle of ketchup and a chunk of cheddar cheese.

During the week, Chandler had been somebody, relatively speaking. As the top reporter for WRT-TV, he commonly presented the lead story on the news. He liked it. He imagined greater things for himself, a network assignment, perhaps, or an anchor position. But then the weekend always came, forty-eight grueling hours of nothing. In a world where most people count the days till the weekend, Chandler counted weekend hours, looking forward to Monday, and another week of dream-making.

It is not an uncommon thought among young TV reporters. Dreaming of the big break is enough to drive them to hard work at low pay—a benefit for news managers who feed the ego if not the paycheck and then report victoriously to the board that once again expenses have been controlled. Reporters, like lottery players, know that something good will happen sooner or later. They are bred to think that way.

He walked aimlessly into the bathroom, looked in the mirror and stroked his hair. He stood for a moment, studying what TV viewers saw. He had good hair—thick, deep brown hair with just enough wave and character of its own to wrap his youthful face perfectly for a TV camera. At thirty-two, he was what television required—according to his bathroom mirror.

Although the demise of the reigning anchorman would provide an opportunity for Chandler, it was not something he thought much about. It simply was not likely. Chandler had established himself as the first-line substitute, but Brady Soles was almost as much a Richmond institution as General Robert E. Lee, whose bronze statue punctuated Monument Avenue. It was sometimes said of Richmond that its most important community leaders had died a hundred years ago. In such a place, any new hero would have to earn his or her place. Chandler's handsome face might draw the favor of a young lady, but it would not, in this town, win him what he really wanted. And certainly not on a Saturday morning. It was his day off, and he didn't want a day off. He retrieved the newspaper from the hallway outside his apartment and flopped into a chair at the kitchen table. A dirty spoon fell to the linoleum as he spread the paper. He would pick it up later. There was no urgency. It was on the floor already. It would do no additional damage.

He glanced over the report of Tisdale's execution, allowing himself momentary amusement in the description of getting Lenny on the gurney. At his death, Lenny Tisdale weighed three hundred seventy pounds. Had his execution been delayed, Chandler mused, it might have been unnecessary; he would have eaten himself to death.

Below the fold, the other big story: the theft of Christmas toys from the Christmas House, a local organization dedicated to creating good cheer in places unaccustomed to it. He knew about that. He also knew that citizens would be so repulsed by the evil deed that they would bring replacement toys to the Christmas House, so that it would have more than it lost, by several times. The theft was therefore, in some sense, beneficial.

He tossed the paper on the floor and walked around the apartment. The stroll was brief. He had been there before. It wasn't the sort of place he wanted to spend Saturday morning—or any other morning, for that matter. Things were different when Sarah was there. The apartment was a suitable place to laze around on a late-December Saturday, but lazing was not his thing. That had been part of the problem. If Sarah were here, the jam-covered spoon on the kitchen floor would be cleaned and in the drawer by now. It wouldn't have been on the floor in the first place. But there were other things that drove them apart. Sarah always encouraged him to get out of bed in the morning for no other reason except that she wanted to make it up. And on those rare days when she was gone before he rose, and returned late at night, she would methodically make up the bed before they climbed back into it. She would tell him not to go to bed until she had made it up. He never fully understood Sarah.

The divorce nearly two years ago had left Chandler with an empty heart, renter's beige walls and the sort of furniture left unsold at the end of a yard sale. From the settlement, he won the right to make up his bed when he wanted to—which wasn't often. It was one of his few victories. But for the most part, it was his career that tore them apart. Too many nights *on assignment* had taken its toll. Sarah had said it in frustration, several times: "You love that damn job more than me."

He brushed his teeth quickly and headed out the door. One more Saturday at the station, he told himself. Then he'd get a weekend hobby. Bowling or carving ducks, perhaps. He unlocked his Saab, climbed in and headed toward the TV station.

The newsroom on the weekend wasn't exactly Macy's on the day after Thanksgiving, but it was better than his apartment. Or the mall. And there was always something to do, even if it was nothing. He drove a couple of blocks and pulled into McDonald's for the standard bachelor's breakfast.

Even that did not go well. He drove in behind three

other cars. He pulled close on the bumper of the car in front of him, as if that would reduce the wait. He was in a hurry to do nothing. Two minutes passed, then his turn came. He didn't even need to glance at the drive-thru menu before ordering.

"I'd like an egg and sausage biscuit," he shouted at the speaker box. "And a large coffee."

"We're not serving breakfast now," a voice said through the speaker box.

"Why not?"

"We stop serving breakfast at ten-thirty."

Chandler looked at his watch: 10:32.

"All right," he said. "I'll just take a large coffee."

The voice squawked a price Chandler couldn't make out, and he obediently pulled forward to pay.

"Two creams and a handful of sugars, please," Chandler said, as he took the coffee.

The expressionless woman in the window silently handed him the cream and sugar. Then she slid the glass door shut and walked away.

"Merry Christmas," Chandler said to the glass.

He pulled up to the road and stirred the sugar and cream into the coffee. Traffic was heavy, and dangerous. Christmas shoppers, in the spirit of giving, raced up and down the pike in total disregard of each other.

As he approached the TV station, Chandler noticed how the neighborhood's respectability went down, block by block. Twenty years ago, when WRT-TV opened its offices on the Southside, it had stood nearly alone on a quiet road. There were few traffic lights and little need for them. Now the city's boundaries lapped at the station itself, and the suburbs had sensibly moved further from the threat of crime that a growing city brings, even when it denies it, as Richmond did.

Convenience stores and flea markets had replaced more significant businesses, and even the local 7-Eleven had closed its doors to be replaced by a nameless convenience store run by a Pakistani family. Chandler could have gotten his coffee there, but he didn't want to risk it. Once, he saw the new proprietor changing chili in the always-on pot behind the hot dogs. The man scraped the gurgling dregs from the bottom, stored it temporarily in a whing-ding cup, poured in fresh chili, then dumped the cup's contents on top. That way, at least, the bottom of the chili pot would always be the freshest, comparatively speaking. Like a grocer rotating stock, the new owner of the old 7-Eleven rotated his chili. But no one ever got to eat the new stuff. The freshening-up process caught it just before it hit the bottom.

The Pakistani man had performed the switch-a-roo methodically in front of Chandler, as if it were routine. It probably was. But there were no bodies lying about the parking lot. The chili couldn't be that bad, Chandler reasoned, unless customers crawled off somewhere else to die. But it was the chili incident that caused Chandler to do his food shopping elsewhere. He didn't spend his money at the Pakistani place after that.

A tall chain-link fence had been put up around the TV station, and brilliant lights illuminated the parking lot—

at most hours of the day. When Chandler pulled into the parking lot, they were burning brightly. It was a sunny morning, but the lights were on anyway.

The automatic sensors had a mind of their own.

Charlie Gladstone sat at the weekend news assignment desk. He was a pleasant kid with pimples, which he would probably outgrow, and a hooked nose, which was likely to stay with him. Charlie might have improved what he had by not wearing his baseball hat backwards or by cutting the lock of hair that he was constantly brushing back from his left eye. But it didn't matter. His chances of becoming a news anchorman were remote, but for a job nobody wanted anyway—sitting in the news room alone on Saturday and Sunday, listening to a row of police and fire monitors squawk—Charlie was well-prepared.

"Welcome to nowhere," Charlie said, looking up from a French textbook. "Did you come in to practice anchoring for next week? I mean, you are filling in for Brady next week, right?"

"Yeah, beginning Tuesday, but that's no big deal. I came in to catch up on the background for the Ragland execution," Chandler lied. "You wouldn't believe how much promotional material an execution can generate when a black governor stands to gain political ground by granting clemency to a white man."

"Especially when he's a rich doctor. I guess that's the major constitutional difference between him and

Tisdale."

"You got that right. What about you—slow day?"

"As usual," Charlie said. "You guys are paying me to do my homework."

Chandler laughed. "In that case, do it well."

Charlie brushed the hair back for the sixth time since Chandler arrived and looked back at his book. Chandler watched the hair slowly fall back over his eye. A monitor screeched irritably, and Charlie turned the volume down without looking.

"You go to church, Charlie?" Chandler asked out of nowhere.

"No. Should I?"

"I don't know. I just asked."

"Do you go?"

"Sometimes, if the music's good."

"Is that the only reason?"

"No," Chandler said. "It's not the only reason. But why go to a church that has bad music?"

"Yeah, I guess. Why are we talking about church, anyway?"

"I'm going tomorrow. I'm speaking to a Sunday School class."

"You get paid for that?"

"Of course not."

"Then why do you do it?"

"Because they asked me to."

"And that's it?"

Chandler shrugged. "Sure. Why not?"

"Sounds like a dud, to tell you the truth. I'd offer to

come hear you, but I've got the desk again tomorrow, unfortunately."

"It pays more than Sunday School speeches."

"Not much more," Charlie said, brushing back the lock of hair, which immediately fell right back where it was.

"What's Wally up to today?"

Wally Figgers, the weekend reporter, was not exactly a candidate for the Pulitzer, but he imagined himself to be. Management knew Wally was not very smart but seemed to think he would overcome it. But Wally had worked weekends three years, and his IQ had not improved noticeably.

"He's got something across the river," Charlie said. "Shopping mall story. He's got another one on this side of the river too, with a mall Santa. After that, he'll sit around and wait for a Christmas tree fire, I suppose."

"Maybe he should take up French."

"Maybe. But he's got to master English first."

Chandler walked back to his desk, thinking about Dr. Ragland sitting on death row anticipating his own death, just short of Christmas. He wondered whether Ragland's last words would be as incisive as those of Tisdale. Ragland certainly had the cultural advantage; perhaps he could top Tisdale's "Merry Christmas."

One of the scanners behind Charlie squawked a message, and, without turning, Charlie shut the volume down. Another scanner kicked in with the same message: A citizen in the West End had phoned police to report an assault.

As Chandler leaped from his chair and ran to Charlie's desk, the dispatcher repeated the message to units in the area. Then the little red diode light on the scanner skipped on to the next channel. Eagerly, Chandler backed it up to the assault channel and waited.

Charlie looked up from his French book. "What is it? All I heard was the assault."

Chandler didn't say anything—and neither did the scanner.

"Did I miss something?"

"Yeah," Chandler said. "That assault was in River Heights."

"So?"

"People don't get assaulted in River Heights," Chandler said. "Especially at ten-thirty on Saturday morning."

"What do we do about it?"

"Keep your ears on the radio. I'm heading over there."

"For an assault?"

"Yeah, for an assault."

"I don't get it."

"I know. But we'll talk about that later. I'll be in touch."

Chandler put the police monitor back on "scan" mode and hurried out of the newsroom. It looked like he might have something to do after all.

3

Chandler wove through traffic on the Turnpike, wishing, as he often did, that he had a siren and a red light he could stick on the dashboard. Then he'd spread the cars like Moses parting the Red Sea. It was a pet peeve; the slowest drivers seem to prefer the passing lane. The right lane is supposed to be for slower drivers, but they rarely use it. Slow drivers like the passing lane. They seem to think they own it, that it was created for them. He was briefly furious, thinking of those who lose their tempers behind the wheel. He understood road rage, without becoming a participant. It took him almost fifteen minutes just to reach the Boulevard Bridge, and then he got hung up in traffic because somebody in a minivan wanted to shoot the breeze with Amos.

To Amos James, an elderly but affable gentleman, collecting tolls at the Boulevard Bridge was more than a job. It was a social event. It never occurred to Amos that he was directly related to the traffic jams which formed at the bridge. He was just being sociable, saying hi and catching up on the latest local chat. Usually, Chandler lingered politely with Amos, but today he watched the minivan for a brief eternity before leaning on the horn. Almost immediately, the driver waved over his shoulder and pulled out of the toll booth. Other cars passed by Amos a little quicker now, fearful of or perhaps grateful for Chandler's horn. Chandler pulled up to the booth.

"Good morning, Mr. TV Man. What brings you across the river this morning?"

"Morning, Amos," Chandler said. "Got to hurry."

He tossed into the tray the collection of nickels, dimes and pennies left over from McDonald's, and before they had settled in the chute, he sped up the incline.

"Go get 'em, Newsman," Amos shouted. Expectantly, he eyed Chandler's contribution. The toll was twenty cents; Chandler had tossed in seventy-three. Amos smiled as he stoked the excess coins out of the pan and dropped them into his pocket.

The river was low, and Chandler could see a mass of bleached-tan stones beneath him, flickering through the railings. Halfway up the hill, his eyes found the trees that grew up around River Heights and sheltered it from the outside world. Somewhere in there, inside that curtain of trees, might lie a useful weekend diversion, he told himself, hopefully. Within moments, he turned onto Cary Street and was greeted by a row of three police cars racing toward him. Quickly, he pulled onto the shoulder and watched the cars zip past. His Saab quivered in their wake.

A fourth cop car pulled off of Lockdale Lane a block away and sped after the other cops. It must have left the scene of the assault, he figured. Chandler considered turning around to follow the speeding cops, but he couldn't find an opening in the traffic. So he drove down to Lockdale and turned into River Heights. He cruised one block with nothing but a few leaves blowing across the road. Then, out of nowhere, an ambulance with flashing red lights rushed past him and disappeared down Cary, in the direction of the Medical College of Virginia—the same way the cops had headed.

That was probably a first for River Heights, Chandler thought. Usually, the residents had the good breeding to die quietly. And none of them left the neighborhood with sirens blaring. Who knows. Maybe the victim would get a stern letter from the River Heights Civic Association, urging him to cease and desist such loud behavior. A cop car turned the corner behind Chandler and passed him in a blur.

Somewhere, the association was already dictating that letter.

Chandler reached for his portable emergency scanner and locked out the other channels, so he could monitor the conversation between the paramedics and MCV. The chatter was urgent.

"We have a white male about fifty with multiple face fractures...apparent assault...blood pressure eighty over fifty, pulse one-thirty. Subject is unresponsive."

Eighty over fifty was bad news, an indication of internal bleeding. The paramedics would put mast trousers on the victim to squeeze blood from the lower extremities to his upper body.

"The patient is becoming combative," the paramedic continued, out of breath. "Trying to sit up. ETA about ten minutes."

Chandler started again to turn and follow the ambulance but changed his mind and continued to the scene of the assault. He was almost there. If it turned out to be nothing, he would go for the other emergency, whatever it was.

A lone police cruiser sat at the foot of the driveway when Chandler pulled up. A woman wearing a baby-blue nightgown and matching robe was being hugged protectively by an elderly man near the foot of the driveway while Lieutenant Glen Robinson attempted to ask questions. Another officer Chandler didn't know stood in the far corner of the yard, interviewing the handful of onlookers.

Robinson, he knew. Robinson was a poster child for the Richmond P.D.—tall, handsome, articulate, African-American. He could have been a movie star, but he chose to be a cop instead. Whenever local news needed a cop for TV, Robinson got the call. Though Robinson never said much and always wore a poker face, Chandler counted him among the better cops to work with. He seemed intelligent, but perhaps it was a ruse. One can often impress others by keeping one's mouth shut.

After glancing at the puddle of blood and glittering tooth fragments, Chandler slipped his press credentials around his neck and climbed out of the car. When the elderly man saw him approaching, he pulled the woman in the bathrobe away, toward the house. Chandler stood alone with Robinson and his notepad.

"Mr. Harris," Robinson said. "Welcome to another routine day in River Heights."

"What the hell happened here, anyway?"

"Somebody beat the crap out of this guy," Robinson said. "Don't know why yet."

Robinson, satisfied that he had said either enough or too much, walked back to his cruiser.

Chandler turned his attention back to the woman in the bathrobe, but as he approached, the elderly man helped her into a car and offered him a threatening look.

"What the hell do you want?"

"I'd just like to ask a few questions," Chandler said.

"Get off this property," the man said.

Then he got in the car and drove away.

For a few minutes, the two cops made a show of going door to door, looking for witnesses. They walked quickly, then left quickly, as if they didn't expect much. Apparently, they got it. After they checked the last house on the block, they jumped into their patrol car and raced off as if they didn't want to be there in the first place. Almost immediately, the onlookers drifted back to their homes. No one bothered with the bloody mess on the driveway. Apparently, the hired help didn't work on the weekend.

Chandler retrieved his cell phone from the front seat and called Charlie at the station.

"Channel 4 News," Charlie said, in a rush. "May I help you?"

"This is Chandler. Grab the criss-cross and tell me who lives at 1619 Lockdale Lane."

"Wait a minute, Chandler. I've got something else going on."

"What?"

There was no answer. Charlie had laid the receiver on the desk. Chandler could hear urgent traffic on the scanners, but he couldn't make out what it was. He hung up the phone and dialed another news number. The phone rang several times. Finally, Charlie answered.

"Damn it, Charlie, don't put me on hold again. Now, who lives at 1619 Lockdale Lane?"

"Okay, okay. I've got an officer down, and Wally isn't answering. I've got to find Wally or my ass has had it."

Chandler started the car and pulled away from the curb.

"Where's the officer down?"

"On Cary," Charlie said. "Where are you?"

"I'm headed toward Cary. How far down is it?"

"At Lombardy."

"I'm on my way. Who's the photog on call?"

"Richard, I think."

"Call him," Chandler said. "He lives five minutes

away. I'll meet him there. We'll find Wally later."

Chandler sped down Cary toward Lombardy. When he arrived, he saw a Channel 4 News car already on the scene. It was Wally. Chandler jumped from his car and ran through the crowd. The other police cars at the scene were speeding away under full siren and lights.

"What happened?"

"A police officer's been shot," Wally said.

"Did you get it?"

"We got everything. The cop pulled somebody over, and the guy just shot him."

"Is he dead?"

"I don't know," Wally said. "They were doing CPR before they put him in the ambulance. I don't think he was breathing."

"Obviously not," Chandler said, "if they were doing CPR."

"Yeah," Wally mumbled. "I guess."

While his photographer continued to shoot tape, Wally wandered about with an unattached microphone, asking questions of people who had no answers.

"Wally," Chandler yelled. "Your microphone's not connected."

"Damn it, Chandler. I'm doing the best I can. Leave me alone!"

"You're doing fine, Wally. But unless you plug the microphone into the camera, you won't have any sound."

"I got here first, damn it. Now get lost. This is my story."

For a moment, Chandler watched Wally rush about with the loose microphone wire whipping around him. Then Chandler walked back to his car and headed toward MCV. Halfway there, he called Charlie to report that Wally had the pictures, if not sound, and that he would stand by at the hospital with more information.

"Meanwhile, give me the name of the unfortunate guy who lives at 1619 Lockdale Lane."

"Sure," Charlie said. "Sorry about the confusion earlier. Let's see…here we go. The name is Philip Jaco."

4

Jaco was in Trauma Two by the time Chandler parked his car illegally in front of the emergency entrance and pushed through the cops lining the corridor. The police officer who had been shot lay in Trauma One, and since that was where most of the attention was directed, Chandler was able to slip into Jaco's surgery by doing little more than lifting his press credentials and waving them at no one in particular.

Almost immediately, he wished he'd waited outside.

There was blood everywhere—on the examining table, on the floor and on the five doctors and nurses who leaned over Phil Jaco with various instruments. His face seemed to have caved in on itself, as if he had somehow swallowed his own teeth, nose and cheeks in one great gulp. What was left wasn't something immediately recognizable as a face.

Two IVs had been set up, and lactated ringers flowed into his veins, but as Chandler watched from the doorway, Jaco's skin went suddenly from the color of a robin's egg to the color of a deep pool in summer.

"Stridor!" the surgeon said.

Jaco, in respiratory distress, wheezed and struggled on the table as blood bubbled from his mouth and nose. He needed air, but the massive facial edema made normal breathing impossible. At the surgeon's order, a second-year resident made an incision under the Adam's apple and inserted a large steel needle, through which air began to enter Jaco's lungs.

Almost immediately, the blue cast to his skin began to disappear, and doctors turned their attention to raising his blood pressure.

"Notice the bloated stomach," the surgeon instructed.

MCV was a teaching hospital, and even in the midst of a crisis, senior staff found opportunity to lecture.

"Internal bleeding," the resident said, quickly.

"So?"

"We need to draw blood for type and cross-match."

"Correct," the surgeon said. "And we need X-rays of the chest and abdomen."

As they swung a camera-and-arm mechanism around for the X-rays, somebody bumped the door against Chandler, and he stepped aside. It was the cop who had been with Robinson at the scene. He stared at Chandler suspiciously.

"Reporter," Chandler said.

The cop frowned and stepped up behind the surgeon.

"Has he said anything?"

"Of course not," the surgeon replied, without looking up.

The cop lingered, fascinated with Jaco's face. "Let

me know if he talks."

The surgeon grunted. The cop walked out.

"Fractured ribs eight through twelve," someone yelled, from across the room.

"I'd like a CAT," the resident said, but the surgeon shook his head.

"No time."

The surgeon picked up a scalpel and, with a short, darting motion, made a small incision under Jaco's navel. Then he inserted a catheter to drain fluid from the abdomen. For a moment, everyone watched the fluid flow through the tube into a plastic bag on the floor. It was pure blood—a liter or more.

Immediately, Jaco's abdomen was opened up, and the surgeon reached in behind the fractured ribs and felt what he suspected: a mushy spleen. It was too badly damaged to save, so he pulled the spleen from behind the rib cage, severed it and shut off the connected arteries.

That's when Chandler walked out of the room.

Lieutenant Robinson sat filling out his report in the waiting room, so Chandler got two cups of coffee from the vending machine and carried them over to Robinson's chair. Captain Brenda Montgomery, chief of the detective division, walked out of the room where the wounded officer lay. She was visibly upset, though she had enough presence to scowl at Chandler as she walked toward the door. They knew each other, but not well. She sometimes showed up at the television station with Robinson for a call-in show, a regular feature of Channel 4. The station often invited police to join the regular volunteer staff to go on the air and invite viewers to call in police tips. It was a useful service that got results. There had even been occasions when wanted criminals would see the invitation to turn in a criminal and call in to report themselves. Robinson watched Montgomery leave the hospital, then took the coffee as if he had been waiting for it. Chandler waited for him to take a sip, and then he asked the obvious question.

"Any theories yet?"

Robinson glanced up and shrugged. "Not really. Could have been a professional job, I guess."

"How so?"

"The guy's face was bashed in by at least two blows that would have broken the attacker's hand if he wasn't wearing protection. Which he had to be wearing. My guess would be a sap glove."

"Sap glove?"

"Yeah," Robinson said. "One of those gloves you can get out of *Soldiers of Fortune*. It's filled with lead pellets. You know, to weight your hand."

"Damn. Not many people have things like that, huh?"

Robinson shrugged. "Some do."

"Then you think it was a contract job?"

"Right off-hand, I'd say: I don't know. How's that?"

"Any witnesses?"

"Nope."

"How's the officer who got shot?"

"Not good. He's on life support," Robinson said, lowering his voice even more.

"Any idea who hit him?"

"None. He didn't call in. Apparently he just pulled the guy. Don't know why. Nothing serious. Didn't even have his book with him."

"Who called it in?"

"A citizen," Robinson said. "He said he didn't see anything, just heard a car screeching, went outside and saw Burke lying in the street."

"Burke?"

"Bill Burke, Patrolman."

"Who was the citizen?"

"The owner of Buddy's Restaurant, just up the street from the shooting."

"I've got a theory," Chandler said.

"Already? What took you so long?"

"The guy who hit Phil Jaco was speeding down Cary Street, and Burke pulled him over."

"Wrong."

"Why?"

"Burke would have called in before he made the stop."

"What if he didn't have time?"

"We have procedures, Chandler."

"Okay. Who called in the Jaco thing?"

"I don't know. A neighbor, I guess."

"You don't think much of my theory do you, Lieutenant?"

"Look, I've got work to do. When you solve the Burke shooting, give me a call. If it's connected to the other thing, I'll say you're brilliant and recommend you for a citizen's plaque or something. Okay?"

"Thanks, Lieutenant. You've given me incentive."

Robinson stood up and joined a group of officers across the room. After writing a few notes in his pad, Chandler glanced at Gloria Jaco. She sat in a beige chair next to the window with a Styrofoam cup of coffee balanced delicately on her knee, as if she were taking tea alone on a slow Saturday morning. After confirming that the protective neighbor wasn't around, Chandler crossed the room and knelt beside Jaco's wife.

"I'm sorry to bother you. My name is Chandler Harris. I'm a reporter with WRT-TV."

"So?" she said coldly, not looking at him.

"I know this is a terrible time to do this," Chandler said, "but I was wondering if I could ask you a couple questions."

She shrugged. "I didn't know you did news on the weekend."

"Yes, ma'am, I do. I mean, we do. Would you spell your husband's last name?"

"J-A-C-O. Just like it sounds."

Chandler scribbled it down on his note pad. "And his age?"

"Fifty-three."

"Occupation?"

"Why do you care?"

"I may be able to help."

She shrugged. "He's president of Family Bakeries."

'Family Bakeries,' Chandler wrote, telling himself he'd never eat their cookies after having seen their president's face.

"How long have you been married, if you don't mind my asking?"

"Forever," she said.

"That's a long time these days."

"You don't need to tell me," she responded coldly. She leaned over the side of her chair and took a cigarette out of her purse.

"I'm going to ask you a few more questions," Chandler said, as she held a lighter up to the cigarette. "They're a little personal, though, and you shouldn't feel a need to answer them, of course."

"Of course," she said, without emotion.

In rapid succession, Gloria Jaco denied that her husband was in financial trouble, was involved with another woman, gambled or socialized with anyone who might be associated with organized crime. She also denied that it was even faintly possible that her husband might be involved with another man. Lieutenant Robinson had asked that, and to hear it again disturbed Mrs. Jaco. It was a thought she had never had.

Chandler stopped the questions for a moment to find her an ashtray—it was a no-smoking area, so she ended up using his empty coffee cup—and then he resumed. She didn't know the details of her husband's finances or business dealings, but she conceded that he was a good person, of sorts.

"Even in recession years," she said, "Phil did not reduce his staff. When times are tough," she added, smiling bitterly, "people still eat cookies."

For a moment, Chandler wondered that the woman who had been in a state of panic a half hour earlier was now capable of sarcasm.

"Thank you," Chandler said. "I guess you have a point." He started to walk away, then turned for one more question. "Mrs. Jaco, you found your husband?"

"Yes."

"Did you call the ambulance for your husband?"

"Yes. But I was a little late."

"A little late?"

"The lady at 911 said she had already gotten the call, and an ambulance was on the way. She told me to relax."

"Did she say who called?"

"No." Mrs. Jaco shrugged and flicked a length of ash into the cup. "She just said the ambulance would be there any minute."

Chandler thanked her and looked around for a pay phone. There was one in the waiting room, but he wanted more privacy. He found a vacant office down the hall and dialed the television station.

"Charlie," Chandler said, after a few rings. "I think we should send Wally over to the assault victim's house in River Heights for some video after he finishes with the cop story."

"It's just an assault, right?"

"Yeah," Chandler said. "But it looks like a professional job, and you don't get those in River Heights. Besides, I think there might be a connection to the cop shooting. It's not out of the way. Wally can snag it on the way back to the station."

"Anything else?"

"No, not at the moment. I'll call you back shortly."

He hung up the phone and headed straight for police headquarters, which was located in the Public Safety building three blocks away. The Police, Fire and Rescue Phone Center filled the basement of the building. Everyone was too busy to notice him, so Chandler walked down the stairs without showing his press credentials to anyone. All that red tape, he thought—going through the process of getting press ID, as if it were for the CIA or something—and nobody wants to see my press pass.

Six or seven phone operators tucked behind partition walls hardly noticed Chandler enter the dark room. As he hesitated, wondering who was in charge, an older man walked out of a corner office.

"May I help you?"

"I'm Chandler Harris with WRT-TV. I just left the hospital."

"How's the wounded officer?"

"Not good, I'm afraid. I think they're just keeping him alive."

"I'm sorry to hear that. Who was—excuse me—who *is* he?"

"Patrolman Bill Burke. That's all I know."

"I don't know him."

"I don't either," Chandler said. "Apparently, he pulled a vehicle over, and the driver shot him when he approached the car."

"Damn!"

For a moment, Chandler stood next to the man and shook his head. Then, as the man started to turn away, Chandler asked him the question he'd come to pose.

"Before Burke was shot, there was an assault in River Heights. I suspect it might be connected to the Burke shooting, but the police don't see it yet. Can you tell me where the River Heights call came from? I mean, I don't want to cause a problem but..."

"No problem."

The supervisor, apparently unruffled by the unauthorized request, walked over to a computer screen and tapped keys on the keyboard. A few seconds later, the information came up on the screen.

"Lockdale Lane, 10:47 a.m., from...the Jaco house. Same place we sent the ambulance."

"Yes, I know. Mrs. Jaco called it in. But she said you—or your operator, rather—told her that it had already been called in. Is there another call listed?"

The supervisor played with the keys some more and called up another screen of data.

"Here we go," he said. "10:34 a.m. Wait a minute."

"What's wrong?"

"This number."

"Yes?"

"It's a pay phone."
"Where?"
"3619 Cary Street, outside of—"
"Buddy's Restaurant?"
"How did you know?"
"I didn't," Chandler said, elated. "I just guessed. Thank you very much, Mr.—"
"Hilton. Jerry Hilton. Used to be a cop myself."
"Is that right?"
"Yeah, I spent seventeen years on the street. Couldn't take it any more. So they promoted me to this basement."
"Were you a detective?"
"Nope. But I solved a lot of cases."
"Mr. Hilton, you may have just solved another one. Thanks for your help."
"Any time Mr.—what did you say your name was?"
"Chandler. Chandler Harris from WRT-TV."
"Do you work with Brady Soles?"
"Yeah. In fact, I'll be filling in for Brady next week."
"I don't like him—I watch Channel Nine, to tell you the truth. But I'll look for you."
"Thanks. Tuesday night. I start Tuesday night."

Chandler hustled back up the stairs and drove toward the TV station. On the way, he called Charlie again and ordered some exterior shots of Buddy's Restaurant, featuring the phone booth outside.

"I'll explain later," he said, before Charlie could ask.

Then he hung up, checked his address book and dialed the number for Robinson's supervisor, Captain

Brenda Montgomery. If Robinson had no imagination, he would go over his head.
 Robinson, he muttered, would be sorry.

5

Montgomery's line rang four times before her voice mail kicked in. Chandler expected that. Montgomery was probably still tied up with the Burke shooting. Chandler left a message, saying he had information that might help with the Burke case and that he would like to discuss it when she was available. Then, on an impulse, he drove back by the scene of the shooting.

The street was still roped off, and three or four police officers milled about. Chandler cruised around the block and then spotted Lt. Robinson coming out of Buddy's and walking in the direction of the crime scene. It struck Chandler as odd that Robinson had gotten there so quickly. Perhaps, he thought, Robinson had reconsidered his theory and wanted to check it out. Chandler pulled back onto Cary and drove back across the river.

Traffic remained heavy, and Chandler had to weave through the cars on the Turnpike. As he approached the station, he called Irv Rafferty, the station's news director. Irv's machine picked up, so Chandler left a message saying he was going to do a cut-in to announce the officer's shooting. Before he'd even crossed the parking lot, Irv called back and ordered him to scratch the cut-in.

Chandler was stunned. "Jeez, Irv. A cop has been shot, probably killed. What are you talking about, scratch the cut-in? We're only interrupting cartoons."

"That's the point," Irv barked. "Only kids are watching. The competition is still asleep, and the only thing we would accomplish is tipping them off. There will be no cut-in!"

Then Irv hung up.

Chandler stormed angrily into the building and sat fuming in the newsroom. He watched the other stations as they ran cartoons without breaking away, except to air commercials for cereal loaded with sugar, sticky candy and other useless products. Chandler wondered why citizens' groups complained about cartoon violence but were strangely silent on the junk kids were putting in their stomachs.

For the rest of the afternoon, Chandler worked the phones, trying without success to dig up more information. Wally strutted around the newsroom while his package was being edited, talking about how he had beat the competition. He made no calls to dig up additional information. He didn't want to have to re-edit his report with late facts. Later, he would return to the scene of the shooting and introduce his package from there, then respond to pre-arranged questions from weekend anchor Bill Nelson. Before leaving the building, Wally went into the bathroom with his makeup kit, cared carefully for his face, then headed out.

The Sunset Lounge

"See you on TV," he announced as he walked out the door, smiling.

By late afternoon, Captain Montgomery had not returned Chandler's call, so he went home.

It was almost five o'clock by the time Chandler pulled into his assigned parking spot in front of the apartment building. Except for the lights in the widow's apartment downstairs, the place looked abandoned. He stepped out on the pavement and locked the door just as the automatic street lamps clicked on. It made the mica flakes in the pavement shine, and for a moment he stared at them and thought about the tooth fragments lying in Jaco's driveway. Then he climbed the front steps and slipped a key into the front door.

Musty air welcomed him home. Before he turned on a light, he reached over and hit the switch on the floor fan. The building's heat was inadequate, and he used an electric heater and the fan to blow warm air around the front room on cold nights. Tonight, though, he just stood in the doorway and let the fan suck fresh air in. After the place smelled a little better, he closed the door and turned on a light.

He walked into the kitchen, picked up the dirty spoon and tossed it into the sink. He planned to wash it later. He checked his answering machine, but nobody had called from the station. Montgomery was ignoring him. He flipped on the TV and roamed through several cable channels. He paused a few moments on the Discovery

Channel to watch a special on the mating habits of giraffes on the Amboseli Plain. Television is so simple, he thought. A camera crew had spent months in Africa shooting film of mating giraffes. Back in the States, someone had written a script, then some guy who had never seen a giraffe went into an audio booth and read the script. It was all edited together, and the voice of authority that explained what was going on droned on as if it were a funeral chant. He wondered whose voice it was. Some over-the-hill anchorman, no doubt, who found work reading scripts. He imagined Brady Soles doing that some day, when he no longer anchored the news. Brady could probably read a good giraffe script.

Chandler's cheap chime clock announced it was six o'clock. He flipped to Channel 4.

The news opened with Nelson reading a voice-over with tape of the scene where the officer was shot. Then Nelson cued Wally on location for a live report. Wally opened with the memorable line, "Thank you very much, Bill." Immediately, Chandler flipped through the other news stations and found them also leading with the story, but they lacked the video of the downed officer being loaded into an ambulance. They, in fact, had nothing except aftermath footage of where the shooting had occurred and interviews with several citizens who hadn't seen or heard anything but were willing to say so. Chandler hated to admit it: Irv had been right to scratch the cut-in.

Wally babbled through his report and then responded to pre-arranged questions offered by anchorman Nelson.

The Sunset Lounge

The actual story was far too brief, considering its significance, but without his mike being plugged in, Wally couldn't have gotten much more anyway. As usual, Wally had warned Nelson not to ask him anything he didn't know, which was a lot. So Nelson thanked Wally for his report, and Wally smiled, which seemed out of sync with Nelson's expression of extreme concern. To Wally, though, it was a moment of great rejoicing. He had done a live report without self-destructing.

Nelson announced that Deborah Manley was standing by at the hospital, and she dutifully reported that the officer's condition was grave, but he was still alive. The news proceeded to more reports on the shooting, with reaction from fellow police officers, most of which had been collected earlier by Deborah for Nelson to read. Deborah's microphone had been plugged in. Those interviewed hailed Burke as a policeman's policeman, a wonderful public servant and a good family man. His family—a wife and two young children—were in seclusion, but neighbors spoke for them.

"There is not," Nelson said ominously at the end of the stories, "one clue to the gunman."

"Yes there is," Chandler muttered.

The assault on Lockdale Lane was not mentioned in the news. Neither was any other crime in the city, all of which were insignificant compared to the Burke story.

Chandler snapped off the TV and looked around at the apartment's twilight gloom. He considered ordering a pizza, but the thought of eating it alone in the apartment was too much. So he decided to combine dinner with detective work and drove back across the Boulevard Bridge to Buddy's Restaurant.

Buddy's was not exactly a four-star restaurant, but it had survived in business for just about ever. It had never been remodeled or improved, the menu never changed, and everyone who went knew exactly what to expect: fair food, familiar clientele. The waitresses, like the food, were plain but reliable.

When Chandler arrived, he glanced approvingly at Cleo Bottoms, who sat at the piano going through his usual rendition of Elvis songs with an occasional imitation of Roy Orbison. At Buddy's, at least, patrons were safe from Jimmy Buffett. Chandler took a booth near the piano because it was the only one vacant. He searched the room quickly, then glanced back to the piano player. Cleo had seen better days and presumed he was still in them. He was as bald as an eagle but thought no one noticed. As long as there was hair on the back of his head, he could invite it to the front for a performance. Fortunately for Cleo and those who listened to him, he could sing fairly well.

Chandler ordered a burger and a beer, and after they came, he signaled for the owner to come over. A moment later, the owner crossed the room, nodding at various patrons, and stopped at Chandler's booth.

"I'm Chandler Harris with Channel 4."

"I thought I recognized you," the owner said, shaking Chandler's hand. "My name's Buddy. How's the burger?"

"Just fine, Buddy. Listen, I want to know something. This morning, when the cop was shot, you called it in."

"Yeah, I was the first on the scene."

"What did you see?"

"Nothing, really. Just the cop on the street."

"You didn't see another car?"

"No."

"What prompted you to walk outside? Did you hear the shot?"

"No, that's the strange thing. I heard noise and thought there was an accident or something. So I looked out and saw the cop car. But no accident. Then, a minute later, when I stuck my head out the door, I saw him on the street with blood pouring out of his head. I ran back in and dialed 911."

"There's a phone booth outside your front door. Did you, by any chance, see anyone use that phone shortly before Burke was shot?"

"No, not that I noticed. But then again, that's not something I would notice."

"Did the police ask you all these same questions?"

"Yeah, they were here before the ambulance was. I told them just what I told you—which isn't much, I guess."

"Buddy," a waitress called out from the kitchen door. "Could I see you for a minute?"

"Sure," Buddy called back. "Nice to meet you, Mr. Harris. Enjoy your burger before it gets cold."

"Thanks—just one more question."

"Sure."

"Did a tall black policeman come back later, Officer Glen Robinson?"

"Yeah, as a matter of fact, he did."

"What did he want to know?"

"Same thing. It was a little strange, though. He was by himself, and didn't take any notes. He just asked questions, then left."

Buddy signaled for a waitress to bring Chandler another beer, gratis, and disappeared in the kitchen. Chandler nursed his new beer and watched Cleo close his eyes and howl. Cleo was into Orbison now, and that required energy.

After he finished the burger, Chandler scribbled some notes for his Sunday School speech on a napkin. It was hard to get his mind on the assignment. Fortunately, he didn't have to plan much because he assumed most of the time would be filled with a question-and-answer session. So with some standard opening comments safely on the napkin, he tucked it in his shirt pocket and finished his beer.

On his way out, he stopped by the piano and told Cleo how much he had enjoyed his singing. Cleo nodded, disrupting the hair architecture a bit, then broke into "Heartbreak Hotel." Chandler dropped two dollars in the glass on the piano and walked out.

He still had some time to kill, so he drove to the mall and watched a film that was so forgettable he forgot the title before it was half over. He got home just in time for the late news. There was no new information on Burke's killer, and Nelson didn't even mention the assault in River Heights. During the first commercial break, he checked his answering machine. No one had returned his call. Apparently, Montgomery had about as much faith in his crime-solving skills as Robinson did.

That angered Chandler. He had worked hard on his day off, and he had tried to assist Wally, but more significantly, he had found a link that might explain the sudden violence in Richmond's West End. Perhaps it was the casual way he was disregarded by the experts in their respective fields that sent him to bed angry. His eyes fixed on the ceiling, Chandler allowed his thoughts to rush beyond the Sunday still to come. He had what he needed to solve a brutal crime and, in the process, make a name for himself.

It was a good thought for a young reporter, but he could not know the danger.

6

Chandler arrived at the large, neoclassical church shortly before ten, wearing a carefully chosen red tie and a somber demeanor that, as he knew from past experience, was appropriately devout.

A plump deacon, grinning too much, greeted him at the door. The deacon extended his hand and exclaimed how glad he was to see Chandler. It was the same greeting he had given the couple who had just entered in front of him. That was his job. Everyone was to be gladly seen. Chandler surmised that the grinning deacon had no idea who he was. There was no special reference to the visiting TV star. The grin was an equal-opportunity grin.

The class session started as he expected. Chandler delivered his speech, made a few comments about how sinful television had become and encouraged anyone who didn't like it to send their comments to the general manager. He also tactfully suggested that viewers could always turn the TV off and read a book if they didn't like what was on it. Then he proceeded to explain how, on balance, television was good, that it had opened millions of minds to new information and ideas. This was not exactly a safe comment, given that this particular group was probably not interested in new ideas. But it was his standard speech. Indeed, the five minutes he had invested in preparation at Buddy's was not even necessary.

Having made his comments, Chandler answered a few questions and, with a couple of exceptions, charmed the small group. Everyone seemed pleased, except for a lady who insisted that the liberal media was out to color the real news with its obsession with the negative.

"Why isn't there more good news on television?" she demanded. "Why?"

Chandler smiled. "What do you mean by 'good news'?"

"You know what I mean," the woman said. "Like our Girl Scouts here spend one day every month visiting elderly people in nursing homes, but you never cover that. Not once has it been on television. Don't you think that's good news?"

Chandler thought a moment, and then offered his stock answer. "I think that's good, but I don't think it's news. Girl Scouts are supposed to do good deeds. If they refuse to do good deeds, then it's news." Chandler smiled gently and hastened to repair the damage. "We cover a lot of stories about good things in the community, but people usually don't tune in to see it, and they rarely remember it when they do see it. What they remember, unfortunately, is usually what they don't like."

One man, inspired by the talkative lady, chimed in

with the suggestion that all the television stations conspired to paint Richmond as the murder capitol of the world. To prove his point, he noted that, on the previous night, all three stations had led with the shooting of Officer Burke, and all had spent entirely too much time on the story.

"Was the shooting of the police officer the only thing that happened in Richmond during the weekend?"

"Pretty much," Chandler said, without mentioning the Jaco beating. "It was the most important thing. The police department and Officer Burke's family think it was pretty important. His two little girls think it was pretty important."

Chandler, fearing the man would fire back at him, then asked other members of the class if they thought the cop killing was overdone. When none did, not even the Girl Scout lady, Chandler suggested that perhaps the coverage was roughly what the situation justified. Chandler was young, but he had enough wisdom not to argue with someone whose mind was already made up, especially in a Baptist church.

He glanced at his watch: ten till eleven. Chandler noted the time, thanked the group for the invitation, good questions and valuable discussion, and prepared to leave. But a problem arose: the class members insisted that Chandler join them for the worship service. He looked helplessly at the group, his eyes locking on the old lady who had scolded him. It occurred to him that dumping out now would be interpreted as bad news. He did not want her to walk out, saying, "I told you so."

The Sunset Lounge

He had intended to slip out between Sunday School and church for a hassle-free breakfast before the church crowds filled the restaurants, but the class members nudged him toward the sanctuary, and before he knew exactly what was happening, Chandler found himself nodding uncomfortably as the class president commented on how useful the discussion was and how Chandler would find the worship service a wonderful experience. There was no tactful escape. The class president walked Chandler down the hall with his hand on his arm, as if he were under arrest. The decision had been made: Chandler would stay for the church service.

Neatly dressed Christians filled the large sanctuary. The few vacant seats were near the front. Like the fans of Cleo Bottoms, no one wanted to be too close to the main event. Chandler slid into the second pew, telling himself that he should have argued less with the lady in the Sunday School class. Enemies, he reminded himself, are of little value. Moments later, the choir in flowing robes glided down the aisle, and the congregation rose to help them sing the opening hymn, "Come, All Ye Faithful."

Chandler sang along without glancing at the hymnal. He knew the words. Instead, he quietly eyed his fellow worshippers. They were salt-of-the-earth types, middle-aged man-and-wife combinations. He wondered that so many churchgoers were so old. Perhaps it was the reality that they were closing in on the last few acts of their lives that made eternity seem more likely than it used to seem.

A few youngsters who weren't overly concerned with Judgment Day squirmed, looking for some way to pass the time. The ones with parental permission sat in the balcony. It was a minor separation from mom and dad, an early suggestion of rebellion. Chandler remembered being in their seats. He imagined he was somewhere between the two extremes and gave a few seconds of thought to just where in-between he was. Like the children, his mind was not properly tuned to worship. Then a late-comer caught his eye.

Watching her walk quietly down the side aisle, he remembered how, in the church back home, the Watkies family always came late, every Sunday. In the eleven years he attended that church, the Watkies had never been on time. He remembered the Watkies because, to him, tardiness was rude, disrespectful of whatever the occasion. He used to argue with Sarah about tardiness. He was always early, and she was always late. She would say that she didn't have time to do whatever they were doing, and he would say she had the same amount of time everyone else had, twenty-four hours a day. It was a hateful, useless thing to say. He thought of the Watkies family as he watched the lady take a seat at the far end of his pew. She had apparently slipped in the side door while the congregation was singing. She wore a long, red dress and a black, wide-brimmed hat that partially concealed her face. The hat alone demanded attention. Except for Easter Sunday, hats rarely come to church anymore. This one occupied the second row.

Chandler wondered if she were as beautiful as she seemed to be. She was young and alone, unusual in that respect for Sunday worship service. For a moment, she turned her head back to the congregation behind her, and Chandler caught a glimpse of her face. Yes, he quickly decided, she was beautiful. But she also looked familiar. He imagined he had seen her somewhere before. Only he couldn't remember where.

The audience stood for another hymn, and Chandler noticed that the mystery lady held her hymnal but did not sing. She seemed to be reading the words to herself, listening to the music but hesitant to participate. The hymn was followed by prayer, and then the congregation sat down. Chandler was by this time totally involved in the lady in red. No one else seemed interested in her, but he was. He felt guilty—this wasn't the proper way to behave in church—but he couldn't help it.

As if she sensed his attention, she turned suddenly and looked directly at him. Their eyes locked for a second. Then she looked away, as if offended. Quickly, Chandler turned his head. He worried that other members of the congregation might have noticed his behavior, and he decided to rejoin the service.

Following a few brief announcements by the associate minister, the congregation rose again for a reading in unison. Chandler looked toward the front of the church, glancing inconspicuously every few moments to his left. By the end of the next prayer, he had forced himself back into the routine of the service and closed his eyes.

"Amen."

The congregation again took their seats, and Chandler ventured one more glance...but she was gone. He looked behind him, but she wasn't there either. Apparently, she had used the last prayer to slip out of the sanctuary, probably through the same side door she had entered. He looked around again, considering the consequences of slipping out himself to find her. But the congregation would take notice. Early departures attract even more attention than late arrivals. So he sat in the pew and waited.

It was, Chandler told himself, a remarkably long service. Following the benediction, he had had enough. He moved briskly toward the exit, claiming to those who intercepted him that he had another appointment and must hurry. The broadly grinning deacon was still there, this time encouraging everyone to come back again. His grin was the same as it had been before Sunday School, possibly bigger now. Perhaps even the deacon was glad the service was over. It was lunch time, and the deacon looked hungry. Chandler said he would come again, then hurried to the parking lot, where he lingered briefly, searching the area for the lady in red. He found what he expected—nothing. So he climbed into his Saab and drove quickly away.

7

The newsroom took little notice Monday morning when Chandler walked in with his breakfast, tossed his keys on his desk and set his coffee down beside the TV monitor. A talk show played on the upper fourth of the screen, with CNN in the square next to it. The two lower squares featured various satellite feeds, most of which were re-feeds from the night before.

"Morning," Frank Jones said, without looking up from his computer screen.

Frank was the six o'clock producer.

"Morning, Frank."

"Coffee?"

Chandler lifted the McDonald's cup and shook his head. "How's Burke?"

"He died last night," Frank said, without emotion, and continued pounding away at his keyboard.

"I'm not surprised. Everyone knew as much yesterday." Chandler reached for the phone and dialed information. "I'd like the number for the Medical College of Virginia's front desk, please."

"Just a moment," the operator said.

He watched as other staff members filed into the

morning news meeting. After a moment, someone answered, and after a brief exchange, she transferred him to another desk, and Chandler asked the nurse on duty for information on Philip Jaco's condition.

"Are you family?"

"Yes," Chandler said, in his most sincere voice. "I'm his first cousin."

The supervisor didn't necessarily believe him but didn't necessarily want to make a point of it either. At the moment, she didn't care. She had fielded questions about Officer Burke all morning. It took her a minute to find Jaco in her records.

"Still critical," she said, mechanically.

Chandler thanked her and hung up.

"Assignment meeting," Woody called out, from the conference room. Chandler rose and joined the others.

Everyone settled around the cheap, walnut-veneered table down the hall from the newsroom, and while he waited, Chandler stared at the world map that consumed one wall. He had often allowed his eyes to wander around the world while enduring ponderous meetings. It had paid off: he knew where Burkina Faso was located or at least where it was when the map was made.

Woody stroked what hair remained on his glistening head and studied his assignment sheet. Woody was a smart, hard-working assignment editor with a curt personality. He relieved stress by smoking too much and pulling at his hair. Chandler theorized that Woody would probably have lots of hair if he would just quit pulling it out, but that was Woody's business.

"Before we do today," Woody said, "let's put tomorrow to rest. The cop's funeral is at two at the Ashe Center, and Irv wants to cover it heavy. Jim will be at the funeral. Ernie and Willie will set up the truck after the noon show. Gerald and Mark will be inside with the cameras. Keith and Don will do the setup and run cables tomorrow morning. We'll go over it again tomorrow. Now—"

"That's kind of strange," Chandler interrupted. "I mean, the guy died last night, and the funeral arrangements are already made?"

Woody turned dour. "He was dead when he hit the street. They just pumped him up for a couple of days to make sure. Life support is a wonderful thing. Dr. Ragland would love to have it about this time tonight. All right, today. Jim, you stay with the investigation and wrap the lead live from headquarters."

"Got it."

"Campbell," Woody said, not looking up from his sheet, as his long fingers roamed across his scalp in search of more hair to tug. "You turn a piece on the family. Go by the house and see if you can tactfully get somebody to talk. If not, spray the area and talk to neighbors. Chuck, Burke is—I'm not sure what number he was—"

"Thirty-seven."

"Great. See if you can dig up some video from past cop shootings and background the thing. Don't forget to include the Tisdale killing. We've got lots of footage of that."

"Right."

"Chandler, why don't you find the cop's best friend and ride with him today. A reaction piece from his co-workers, something like that. Susan, why don't you—"

Chandler objected. "Are we doing the whole show on Burke?"

"Pretty much," Woody said, glancing at Chandler. "That and the Ragland execution."

"I've got an idea," Chandler said. "The assault in River Heights—it was reported by someone from a phone booth that just happens to be up the street where Burke was killed. Did you guys know that?"

Everyone looked at him, but no one said anything.

"What if the guy who assaulted Jaco was the same one who shot Burke? Like that's the reason he shot him—he panicked."

Woody shrugged, unconvinced. "At this point, there's nothing to connect the two except for a phone call you say was made from a nearby phone booth. If we turn that speculation into a report and the police do get something, we write ourselves off. Let's cover what we've got. You can play detective later."

"I know, but what if—"

Woody cut him off. "We can't chase what-ifs today. I need you for the reaction piece."

"I could ask some questions," Chandler said. "I might find a cop who would give us a sound bite to base the piece on."

"Forget about it. I've got one reporter left, and Marlo has to cover the Ragland execution tonight. You do the cops' reaction piece, then Marlo tells us about Roger Ragland's last day on earth."

Before Chandler could object again, Irv Rafferty walked in. Already, at nine-thirty, his shirt was wet with perspiration around the neck and under the arms, and he wheezed slightly from the walk down the hallway.

"Morning, everyone," he said, grudgingly. "What are we doing on Ragland?"

"Marlo's watching it," Woody said. "She's set to keep up with the last-minute appeals, then standby with the live truck to head down for the execution tonight—though I'm not sure it's worth the trip."

"It's an interesting case," Irv said, plopping down in a chair against the wall and walking it toward the table. "There's no smoking gun. He might get a break, and we need to keep that possibility alive."

"What are you suggesting?"

Irv leaned across the table. Marlo leaned back to make room and almost fell out of her chair. Those already with their elbows on the table slowly leaned back as well, but not as far.

"I just talked to Ragland's lawyer," Irv said.

He looked around the table as if seeking approval for taking an active part in the news. His big bloodshot eyes darted from side to side, soliciting reaction. One of Irv's eyes was fake, a glass eye. It never moved, but it was bloodshot like the other one. No one was really sure where he was looking. Everyone sat without comment.

"Ragland is available for a live interview from death row," Irv said. "He's only offering it to us. It would fit right into our violence theme tonight, and it wouldn't take a reporter off the street."

Chuck, a reporter unofficially tenured by his twenty-two years on the air, snorted. "Come on, Irv. What would we ask him that we haven't asked before?"

Before Irv had a chance to respond, he noticed Alicia Morgan, the six and eleven o'clock co-anchor, standing in the doorway. She'd been with the station just two years, but she was aggressive and bright enough to deserve her hallowed position as the first top-rated, black female anchor in Richmond, and Irv knew it. She did not hesitate to challenge her boss.

"Why spend any of our resources on a story that will end as expected and have no follow-up?" she asked. "Besides, I don't recall you doing the same thing for Len Tisdale, our previous dead person, who just happened not to be a white doctor."

"That's not the point," Irv stammered, without looking at her. He looked directly across the table as if he were responding to Chandler, or so it seemed. "The point is that Ragland has a damn good argument—which Tisdale did not have. This is his last day, the governor could reverse it and—well, he's available for a live shot on the evening news. So let's do it."

He rose, took on the air of stalwart purpose, rapped his knuckles on the table-top and strode out of the room.

"Ernie," Woody said, with resignation. "When you

finish here, take Livesky to Jarrettsville. We're going to have a satellite shot from the end of the world. Damn. So where were we? Oh yeah. Elaine, what have you got for us?"

Everyone turned to Elaine Winston, sitting quietly at the corner of the table in a salmon-colored dress suit. She'd been awarded the position as "4 News for You" reporter, chiefly because she was a good, hard-nosed reporter, the public liked her, and nobody else wanted the job. It was something the station started ten years earlier and now protected as its most valuable asset: an investigative team supported by a group of volunteers who went to bat hundreds of time each week on behalf of private citizens in trouble. It was the same group that worked closely with the police department in finding wayward criminals. Elaine smiled confidently as she began to speak.

"Today's 4 News for You," she said, "is called 'Give Me Back My Home.' It features a lady in Ashland who was evicted from her apartment because she didn't pay her rent."

"Why didn't she pay her rent?" Woody bated.

"She's got problems," Elaine said, with concern in her voice.

"Obviously," Woody said. "I do too. But I pay my rent."

Elaine bristled. "Woody, I don't need this."

Shawn Dibble, one of the volunteers who worked with Elaine, happened by the door and heard the conversation. He stuck his head in and asked if there was a problem.

"No problem," said Woody. "We're just a bit tight about the Burke thing."

"Good," said Shawn. "I just overheard the conversation and thought I'd ask. We worked real hard for that lady in Ashland."

"No problem, Shawn," Woody reassured. "The piece runs tonight as planned."

"Good. Thanks, Woody. I didn't mean to stick my nose in."

"Forget it. It's okay."

Woody was irritated that a non-staff member would presume to play a part in the news meeting, but he knew the value of the 4 News volunteers and did not want to upset Shawn. As everyone filed back into the newsroom, the main doors opened suddenly and, with a flourish worthy of a screen starlet, Brady Soles, veteran anchorman of Channel 4, strutted across the newsroom.

8

Brady didn't normally come to work in the morning, but sometimes he stopped by. No one paid any attention, though, because Brady's arrival meant only that he had come to work. It didn't mean he was going to do any work.

"Hey, Chandler," teased Woody. "Why don't you ask Brady to read your Jaco story tonight?"

The newsroom responded with scattered chuckles. At the same time, a group of college students touring the station entered the newsroom. Seeing them, Brady underwent a transformation. From irritability, he shifted to fatherly concern.

"There he is!" one of the students whispered.

Brady acted as if he didn't hear. He lingered long enough to be admired but did not get so close to the group that he would be called on to speak with them. Without a script, Brady felt unarmed, so he avoided the crisis by moving with purpose toward the coffee machine, where he graciously offered Chandler a slight nod.

"Morning," he mumbled.

"Good morning, Brady. Got any special plans for the

rest of the week?"

Brady's vacation would begin Tuesday, a bookkeeping thing that rounded out four comp days left unused in the calendar year.

"I'll probably work on the tan a little, if I can find some sun," he said, nonchalantly. "Do some Christmas shopping, read a few books, nothing big."

Brady did not read books and had the knowledge to prove it, but Chandler let the comment slide.

"I'll keep the chair warm while you're gone," he teased.

"Oh—you pulled the short straw?"

"Afraid so."

"Well, don't look too good." Brady forced a smile. "Anything happening today?"

He was obviously unaware that Burke had died, and Chandler wondered if he knew about the shooting at all.

"We're working the Ragland execution," Chandler said, deciding he should let Brady take his own time stumbling over the Burke story. "Nothing groundbreaking, I suppose."

"No doubt," Brady said with authority, and retreated to his office.

Moments later, Irv emerged from his office and announced that the Ragland interview was on for the noon show as well as the evening news.

For a moment, Woody merely gawked, disbelieving. "What?"

"I agreed to put Ragland on the noon news," Irv said. "Is there something wrong with that?"

"Yeah," Woody said. "There's something wrong with that. Jarrettsville is an hour from here, and the satellite truck is still sitting in the garage."

"Well, get Ernie in the truck and tell him to haul ass down there. Ragland's attorney will meet him at the gate. We don't need Marlo on it. Angie can do the interview from the set."

"Angie!"

"Yes, Angie."

"Jeez, Irv," Woody said, as the newsroom stopped to watch the argument. "Before we so wisely scooped her up and announced that she was a journalist, she sold condoms for a living. Do you honestly think she can ask a question?"

"She's our noon anchor," Irv said, though his response impressed no one. "We'll write down some questions for her, if necessary."

Then he strolled to his office and slammed the door.

Between jobs, Angie had recorded public service announcements recommending safe sex. The spots, paid for by the Department of Health and Human Services, suggested the use of condoms for young people who couldn't handle abstinence. The other stations in Richmond ran the spots frequently, to the dismay of Channel 4. But Angie was Irv's find, and he stood by her. The question was, where did Irv find her? The answer: in a bar one night, when Irv was drunk enough to play his role as news director to excess and promise Angie things she would require him, at the point of blackmail, to deliver. Irv accepted Angie as promised and made the best of it. She was pretty, but lacking between the ears. She anchored the low-rated noon show because in that position she would do the station the least damage yet still think herself a star. Angie did not understand ratings books.

Captain Brenda Montgomery sat in her office, frowning at nothing in particular, when Chandler knocked on her door.

"Got a minute?"

"Not really," she said, not smiling. "What can I do for you?"

"I was just wondering if Robinson talked to you. I mean, about what he and I discussed."

"We talked, but not about you. Unless you mean the Jaco thing. Sorry I didn't return your call, but I've been busy."

"I don't doubt it. But now that I've got you, I think you'll be sorry you ignored me, Captain. I've got a few facts you might be interested in."

Montgomery stood up and closed the door to her office and settled back in the leather-bound mahogany chair behind her desk.

"Let's hear it."

"Well, you know that the manager at Buddy's Restaurant called in the Burke shooting."

"Of course, we do," she said, irritably. "Is there anything else I need to hear again?"

"Yeah, Brenda. There is."

She leaned forward. "I'm listening."

"The call about Jaco was made from the pay phone outside Buddy's. A few minutes later, Burke was shot—not a block and a half away."

"How did you know about the call?"

"I checked my sources over at the Public Safety Building."

For a moment, Montgomery stared at the stack of paper on her desk.

"You've got admit it, Brenda. It's a connection you didn't make. You didn't make it, did you?"

She shrugged. "Of course, we did. Look, Chandler, we're up to our collective asses on this thing, and there's very little to go on. It's entirely possible that whoever shot Burke had driven from River Heights. But until we can get something that identifies him, we can't do a lot."

"You've talked to Phil Jaco?"

"Of course."

"He was no help?"

"Not especially."

"Is he afraid of something?"

"Who knows," she said. "He says he just wants to get well and go back to making cookies."

"Was there any evidence left at the Burke scene?"

She shook her head. "Nothing."

They sat for a moment, not speaking. Chandler watched her face. Montgomery looked much older and more somber than she had just a year ago, before her promotion. Still, she was attractive, in a police sort of way.

"I'm not trying to annoy you," Chandler said. "But..."

"It's all right," she interrupted. "I appreciate you trying to help us. But here's the problem I'm having with your theory. The suspect shot a police officer without batting an eye. Why didn't he shoot Jaco too? Except for the coincidence of the phone call, your theory doesn't wash."

"Unless the obvious is what happened."

"The obvious?"

"Sure. He beat Jaco but didn't want him to die. That's why he called for an ambulance."

"Chandler, you're a good newsman, but I'm afraid we can't use you in Homicide. We rely too much on evidence here. You know what I mean?"

Chandler smiled with resignation and stood up. "Thanks, Brenda, but don't give up on me. I've still got some bushes to beat."

"Beat them carefully, Chandler. Or if you'd like a better idea, why don't you do your job and let the police do theirs?"

"Thanks, Captain. I'll be in touch."

For nearly two hours, Chandler wandered about the building, engaging uniformed officers in non-productive chat about Officer Burke. Everyone was shaken by the killing, but few felt inclined to talk about it. At noon, he walked down to the press room and turned the TV set to channel four.

The Sunset Lounge

Other reporters began to gather. After a lead story saying there was nothing new on the Burke killing, anchorwoman Angie Davis smiled and said "in other news," then led her viewers to the Roger Ragland execution. Surprised at the prospect of a live death row interview with the renowned condom lady, the reporters glanced at Chandler and grinned knowingly. For a moment, as his heart sank, Chandler considered slipping out of the room before the blood started to flow. But before he could reach the door, Angie tossed the first stupid question.

"Dr. Ragland, are you ready to die for killing your wife?"

"I did not kill my wife," Ragland said angrily. Like Angie, he was dressed in orange, if somewhat less tastefully. "And I can prove it."

It didn't occur to Angie to ask him how he could prove it. Instead, she skipped over the second question on her list and decided to work up from the bottom — just to show her co-workers she could make decisions.

"Dr. Ragland, you have twelve hours to live — actually you have less than that now." She glanced at her watch and tried to work out the math but gave up after a moment. "How do you plan to spend your last hours?"

Ragland ran a hand through his thick black hair and shrugged at someone off-camera. "I'd rather talk about my case," he said. "I was not at home the night my wife was killed. I have an alibi, and if I'm given a chance, I can prove where I was that night."

Angie nodded her head for a moment, seeming to

weigh the justness of the answer, and then she asked another question off the cuff. "Tell me, Dr. Ragland. Have you ordered your last meal, and can you tell us what it will be?"

Chandler gasped and turned to face the other reporters. "Not us," he stammered. "She doesn't work for us. That's not my station."

"That's what happens," one of the reporters said, "when you make an anchor out of a condom lady."

As the press room enjoyed a laugh at Chandler's expense, Ragland continued to insist that he had been set up—that he had not, in fact, whacked his wife with the fireplace poker that was later found in the backyard with her blood and his fingerprints all over it. Angie continued not to hear him. In the middle of his last statement, as he was claiming that a witness had perjured himself, Angie interrupted.

"I'm sorry, Dr. Ragland," she said, smiling like a chipmunk. "Our time is up. Thank you for being with us on the noon show today."

Before the reporters could stop laughing and start lobbing jokes his way, Chandler grabbed his notepad and a few pens off a side table and headed out for a day with Officer Phil Melano.

9

Sergeant Phil Melano had not wanted to talk to the media. But Melano respected Chandler, so they met in the parking lot of the Third Precinct Headquarters and, after a brief conversation in which Chandler urged him to allow his cameraman to record his comments, all three climbed into Melano's patrol car. The cameraman sat in the passenger's seat so he could get shots of Melano talking. Chandler sat in back.

"Before you ask," Melano said, after starting the car and pulling up to the road, "I have no idea who killed Burke. Bill was gone when I got there. It was just a matter of going through the formalities of trying to save him."

"I understand," Chandler said. He watched traffic part for the cruiser. Melano wasn't chasing anyone, but everyone seemed to have a guilty conscience. Or maybe it was because Melano was speeding. Jeez, Chandler thought: I need a cop car. "Was there anyone standing around who might have seen something?"

Melano shrugged and squealed onto a side street. "Lots of people were standing around, at a safe distance. None of them saw anything or would admit to it."

"Was there anything at the scene? Car tracks—anything?"

"We looked at everything, and found nothing that made any sense. There was no sign of stress at the scene. Bill's car was parked at the side where it would have been for a totally routine traffic stop."

"In other words, the guy shot Burke and then calmly drove away? Didn't spin the wheels or anything?"

"I guess not," Melano said. "But not necessarily. Some tires spin without making noise or leaving rubber. We just don't know."

Melano accelerated around a rusted-out Volkswagen Rabbit and surged toward a red light. After the light turned green, he looked in his rearview mirror and turned left.

"It's normal procedure for a cop to radio in the tag before he approaches a car, isn't it?" Chandler asked.

"Normally, yes."

"Why didn't Burke make the call?"

Melano shrugged and shook his head. "I don't know. I guess it wasn't a threatening situation. It was probably a minor stop. Maybe he knew the guy and stopped him to say hello. Hell, I don't know."

He reached over and hit the siren for a short blast. The sound startled Chandler.

"What's up?"

"Lady made an illegal U-turn," Melano said, pointing to the gray Volvo in front of them. "It was probably something like this that got Burke killed."

"Maybe."

The Sunset Lounge

Melano followed the car over to the curb.

"At least she responded meekly," Chandler said.

"She doesn't want a ticket," Melano said. "The smart ones work with you."

Chandler watched Melano take his hat from the dashboard and step out of the car. The driver in front of them glanced back and waited. Melano stayed back behind the driver as they spoke, out of reach. A minute later, Melano tipped his hat and walked back to the cruiser. As he opened the door, the other car pulled back into traffic.

"No ticket?"

Melano shook his head. "On her way to church with Christmas wreathes. Missed her turn and didn't see the sign."

"But you didn't know that before you pulled her, and you didn't call in before you got out of the car. You violated the basic rule you just explained to me."

"Yeah, I know. But this was not a threatening situation."

"How so?"

"It was a little old lady in a Volvo."

"A little old lady in a Volvo?"

"Yeah. An officer knows when there might be a threat, and clearly this wasn't one."

"Burke's killer might have been a little old lady in a Volvo."

"I don't think so."

"Burke didn't either."

Melano didn't respond. He cut the lights off and

looked over his shoulder. Immediately, cars switched lanes to make room for him. They drove around for a while, watching traffic. Nothing big happened. A call came in for an accident a couple blocks away, but another patrol car had it under control before they got there.

"Good, we got here late," Melano said, passing the accident and waving at the hapless cop in the middle of the intersection. "I hate directing traffic. Seen enough?"

"Sure."

That's the way it is, Chandler thought: routine, most of the time. Most days are the same, then a cop begins to think they are the same and gets careless. Burke was a victim of his own casual routine. They drove back to headquarters, and Melano pulled up beside Chandler's Saab. Fishing for a quote he did not yet have, Chandler asked a couple of questions about what it was like to work with Burke, but Melano didn't seem to want to say much. His comments were brief—one- and two-word answers. Hard to make a sound bite out of them. Which was unusual. Normally, cops rave about a fallen comrade. He probed Melano more, asking some of the same questions he had already asked, hoping for a better answer. He didn't get it. Eventually, he decided to call it quits.

"Thanks, Phil," he said, holding out his hand. "I know this is tough for you."

"Yeah, it's tough." There was a decided lack of emotion in his voice.

"And from what you say, the son of a bitch will prob-

The Sunset Lounge

ably never be found."

"It may not have been a son of a bitch."

"What do you mean?"

Melano hesitated for a moment while the cameraman climbed out of the patrol car and carried his equipment over to his own car.

"I shouldn't be telling you this," Melano said, in a lowered voice. "But I will. It's probably unrelated anyway. Over against the curb beside Burke's patrol car, one of our officers picked up a tube of lipstick."

"Lipstick?"

"Yeah. There's a chance it might have fallen out of the killer's car, assuming the killer was even in a car. We don't know that for sure. Anyway, it was lipstick with a real fancy case. It was so fancy, with raised engraving and so forth, that we couldn't pull prints off of it."

"But that's a residential neighborhood," Chandler said. "The lipstick could have fallen out of anybody's purse."

"It could have, and it probably did. But it's the only thing we found."

"Is there any reason to believe the killer opened his—or her—car door?"

"We think so," Melano said, eyeing the cameraman waiting for approval to leave. "Bill was lying just ahead of his own front left fender. We think the shooter might have stepped out of his car and shot before Bill even got to him. Bill fell straight back beside his own car."

"Why didn't he draw his gun when he saw the driver

coming toward him?"

"Good question."

"You're thinking—"

"I'm thinking if the driver was a woman, Bill might have not felt threatened. He was a smart cop, no matter what others might say. If a man had come toward him, he would have been ready."

"Some people didn't like Burke?"

"Some people. But he did his job."

"Dumb question—what color was the lipstick?"

"Red. Deep, dark red. Nothing subtle about it."

"Thanks, Phil. I'm sorry. If there's ever anything I can do—"

"One thing," he said, holding his hand up. "I know you're a reporter, but this conversation was confidential—I mean, the part about the lipstick. If the lipstick is mentioned on TV, we'll both know where it came from."

"It won't be."

Chandler drove back to the TV station, prepared his report and two hours later went back to the police station to wrap it live. He made no comment to anyone about the lipstick. When his report was over, he drove home, fashioned a dinner of sorts and fell asleep on the couch.

He woke up in time for the late news, heard once again that there was no suspect in the Burke killing, endured a re-cut of his report on Melano and waited as

Brady urged viewers to stay tuned for the latest on the execution of Roger Ragland. In the second block, Alicia tossed to Marlo at the State Pen, but she had no word yet on the execution. Brady thanked her and urged viewers to stay tuned. They bumped across to weather, then sports. Still, there was no word on Ragland.

Following the final story of the newscast, Brady smiled stiffly and said goodnight. Alicia had the presence of mind to add that there was still no word on Ragland. Then, as the camera went to a wide shot of the studio, Brady and Alicia pretended they were chatting with each other. For a few moments, Chandler lay on the couch and watched Jay Leno tell bad jokes well. Then he called the TV station. Alicia picked up.

"So any word on Dr. Ragland?"

"He just died," she said.

"Why didn't he die earlier?"

"Apparently, the governor delayed the execution until he got the last word from the Supreme Court."

"I thought we had done that already," Chandler said.

"We had. But there was some last-minute argument which the Court decided it wanted to hear after all. By the time the governor got the green light and relayed the message to the pen, we were out of time."

"Did the good doctor have any last words?"

"Yes. He said he was innocent."

"Wow, that's creative. I guess he didn't want to compete with Tisdale's 'Merry Christmas.' Do you think he was innocent?"

"What does it matter?"

"Well," Chandler said, flipping the channels idly, "it matters because if he was innocent, he should not have been executed."

"Look, Chandler. I knew the guy, and he was not a nice person."

"You knew Dr. Ragland?"

"Yeah, kind of."

As they talked, Chandler continued to push buttons on his remote control. A man wrestled a snake on one of the educational channels. Chandler lingered long enough to see the man pin its head down on the ground. "How did you know him?"

"I just met him once, that's all. He hit on me."

"So? You're a beautiful woman. You should be accustomed to being hit on. It's hardly a reason to kill a guy."

"I'm just saying I had a bad feeling about him. His wife was six feet away from us, and he...asked me out in the most vulgar way. The way I figure it, anyone who would cheat on his wife so brazenly would do anything he could get by with. It's like stealing—someone who would steal a dime from you would just as readily steal a thousand dollars, if they thought they wouldn't get caught."

"And based on that, you believe he killed his wife?"

"No. I believe he *could* have killed his wife. He had the capacity to do anything he figured he could get by with. He obviously wasn't fond of her. You didn't hear the things he said to me, Chandler."

"You're right. I didn't. I'll see you tomorrow."

"Hey, Chandler."
"Yeah?"
"Remember the words of St. Paul."
"I try to, but sometimes they slip my mind."
"*As a man thinketh in his heart, so is he.*"
"St. Paul was a sharp dude, but I think that's from Proverbs."
"Don't try to ridicule me, Chandler. I respect your religion, whatever it is. You should respect mine."
"I'm sorry, Alicia. What you said makes a lot of sense...more than anything else I've heard today. Goodnight."
"Goodnight, Chandler."
Chandler lay on the couch and stared at the ceiling. For a while, he mused over what Alicia had told him. She was smart, incisive. The quote from Proverbs, twenty years after he first heard it, finally made sense. And it came casually, from a co-worker, as a result of an execution.

Sometime after midnight, still dressed in his office clothes, Chandler fell asleep thinking of what Alicia said.

10

Chandler woke the next morning with one monumental decision to make: whether to wear a gray suit with a yellow tie or a blue suit with a red tie. It was guest anchor day, an event for which he had waited eagerly. After debating the choice, he went with the blue suit and red tie. From there, everything was less stressful.

At one o'clock, he had his hair trimmed. At two o'clock, mimicking Brady, he showed up in time to collect his mail and sit around, sipping coffee. He had not dropped by the morning news meeting. Watching everyone else scramble for stories, he felt powerful. There was no requirement that he bring something to work, like a story idea. All he had to do was look good. It was a pleasant routine. The occasion all but eliminated Philip Jaco from his agenda.

When show time came and he sat in the studio with the cameras staring back at him, the routine Chandler had eagerly anticipated suddenly seemed less easy. He got a small case of butterflies and tried to think about anything but the studio and its quiet, unreal atmosphere. Three times, he reached under the desk and grabbed a stage mirror to check his appearance. With a wet finger, he tamed a few wild hairs which had been revealed by the harsh studio lights. He straightened his tie and pulled his coat tail under his bottom so the collar wouldn't ride up behind his neck as he leaned forward toward the camera. Then he checked the TelePrompTer.

"Can you adjust the white level on the TelePrompTer?"

The floor director shrugged. "You want it up or down?"

"Up."

"Is that good?"

"Thanks."

Beside him, Alicia checked her makeup and moistened her lips. Then, as she dropped the mirror under the desk, the floor director barked, "Stand by!"

Chandler stared into the camera for a moment, glanced at the TelePrompTer and prepared to read. But Alicia, being senior to him, had the first story. She voiced over footage of Officer Burke's funeral and cut to Chuck with a stand-up from the burial site. Then Chandler read a follow-up on the mayor speaking out on violence. He was against it. The show went smoothly. That calmed Chandler's nerves and increased his confidence. At the first commercial break, he tried to break the ice with Alicia.

"Was it good for you?"

"I've had better," she said. "And I've had worse."

"I'll try harder in the second block."

"Don't fake it."

"Brady fakes it."

"Brady's Brady," she said, checking her hair in the mirror. "And you aren't."

"There's much to be thankful for, isn't there?"

Alicia ignored him.

"Stand by!"

During the sports break, Irv came into the studio, looked at Chandler and said nothing—which was a relief. Failure to attract a rebuke from Irv was considered a compliment.

The next morning, after choosing a blue suit with stripes and a new red tie for his second day as anchor, Chandler drove to McDonald's for what he swore would be his last drive-thru breakfast. In the newsroom, he nodded at a few reporters and made his way, as always, toward the office coffee pot. Woody was already making a second pot, but there was still enough in the bottom to fill Chandler's mug. Woody watched him, disbelieving.

"You're going to drink that?"

"I just hope it doesn't take the glaze off the mug," Chandler said. "Anything up today?"

Woody laughed and shook his head. "We're doing a special 4-You call-in for Officer Burke," he said. "You and Alicia will anchor it. The cops want to shake out a witness."

"What time?"

"Five o'clock. We'll have cops on the phones, mostly. You and Alicia stand there looking cute but con-

The Sunset Lounge

cerned and urge viewers to call in tips."

"Sounds good." Chandler tried the coffee and winced. "Maybe I should have waited for the new pot. Anything else?"

"Let's see...oh yeah. Did you hear about Nick Flynn?"

"Who's Nick Flynn?"

"Come on, Chandler. You've met him, with Irv. Don't act like you don't like naked women."

"You mean the guy from the Sunset?"

"Yeah, Chandler. The guy at the Sunset."

"So, what about him?"

"Somebody killed him last Saturday night."

"What?"

"Apparently he was robbed coming out of the Lounge."

"How did he die?"

"They beat him to death."

Chandler set his coffee mug down and stared at Woody. "Beat him to death?"

"Sure," Woody said. "It's quieter, and it saves bullets."

"Has anyone been charged?"

"No," Woody said.

"Are we doing anything on it?"

"It's too old."

"Why didn't we report it when it happened?"

"Because we had the Burke murder. This one didn't make a ripple. Actually, to be honest, we didn't know about it. It's the price we pay for letting Charlie have a

Saturday night off. Charlie alleges he had a date, and if true, it was a major event. But we didn't cover that either."

Chandler carried his coffee back to his desk and sat down without drinking it. Nick Flynn. Beaten to death. Strip joint. Robbery. He picked up the phone and called Brenda Montgomery.

On the fourth ring, her voice mail answered. He left a message asking her to get him whatever information she could from Nick's police report. A half an hour later, she called back.

"You're never satisfied, are you, Chandler? First, you want to tell me who killed Burke. Now you're on Nick Flynn. Are there any other cases you want to solve while I've got you on the phone?"

"I'm working on it," he said. "What can you tell me about Nick?"

"It looks like a simple robbery," she said. "Nick had his nightly deposit in a bag under his arm, and he was apparently walking to his car when he was approached."

"And they beat him to death?"

"Yeah," she said. "Apparently."

"Did they use a sap glove?"

"A sap glove?"

"Yeah. Like with Jaco."

"I don't know about that."

"That's what they used on Jaco—a sap glove."

"Okay. Maybe they did. If so, the connection is unusual."

"I'll say."

The line was quiet for a moment.

"Want some advice, Chandler?"

"Always."

"Do what you do best, let the police do their job, and stay away from the Sunset."

"Why?"

"It's a bad place. A lot goes on there, none of it good. You will come up on the short end of the stick if you hang there."

"I'll keep that in mind. By the way, has Jaco said anything significant yet?"

"No."

"I think I'll pay him a visit."

"Chandler, you're not listening to me. Are you aware of the thin line between investigative reporting and interfering with an active police investigation?"

"Brenda, I can't thank you enough for your help. And if you were listening, you might need less of it."

"Forget it, Chandler. I'm too busy anyway. I've got a cop killer to find. Have a nice life."

Chandler hung up the phone and stared at the ceiling, considering. Then Irv walked out of his office with an un-lit cigarette dangling from his mouth.

"Hey, Irv," Chandler called out. "I just heard about your friend Nick Flynn."

Irv stopped in his tracks. "Yeah, so what?"

"Easy, Irv. Wasn't Nick a friend of yours?"

"Okay." Irv took the cigarette from his mouth and grimaced. "I heard somebody killed Nick, but no one I know is surprised. He was scum."

"You seemed to like him."

"I'm nice to everybody. Nick just happened to own the Sunset and I just happened to run into him from time to time."

"You don't seem broken up about this."

"I'll get over it."

"Thanks, Irv. You do care."

Irv stuck the cigarette back in his mouth and crossed the room. As always, before opening the door and stepping outside, he lit the cigarette and let an acrid puff of tobacco and sulfur fill one corner of the newsroom. He could have as easily lit it outside, but he always cheated just a step, perhaps in unconscious protest of the no-smoking policy. Then, in strict conformity with the policy, he stepped into the parking lot. A moment later, Frank called everyone to the assignment meeting.

Chandler followed the others, but his thoughts wandered. The addition of Flynn to his list of unsolved mysteries scared him. He was more convinced than ever that there was something going on which exceeded the superficial grasp of his news organization. And it bothered him just a little that he was the only one interested in it. After the meeting ended, he told Frank he'd be back later. Then he drove to the Medical College of Virginia. He had delayed long enough.

11

The receptionist working the front desk seemed new to the job. Chandler didn't think you could smile that pleasantly after spending a few years watching people die. He showed her his credentials and asked directions to Philip Jaco's room.

"He came in this past Saturday," Chandler said. "Assault victim."

They shared a smile while she looked for the name.

"Second floor, room two-forty-two," she said. "But he's not supposed to see visitors yet, unless they're family."

"Would you believe I'm his cousin?"

She smiled. "No."

"Does he ever get visitors?"

"Just his wife, and an occasional police officer. Actually, the police come more than his wife does."

"Is anyone here now?"

"No, the police just left. His wife might come, though. This is about the time she comes."

Yet more smiling.

"You said the police were just here?"

"Yes."

"Who?"

"I don't know. They come, they go. I don't really pay any attention because they never stop at the desk."

Chandler thanked her and walked to the elevator. As the doors closed, he saw she was still smiling at him. As he stepped onto the second floor, a nurse at the nurse's station stopped him.

"You look familiar," she said.

"I look like everybody's uncle," Chandler called back, not slowing down.

"No," she said. "Really. Aren't you on TV?"

That made him stop.

"I watch you guys every night," she said. "It's so funny, the things you say."

"What a nice compliment," Chandler said. "What's your name?"

"Lisa. Lisa Pointer."

"Nice to meet you, Lisa."

"That woman you're with—what's her name?"

"You're probably thinking I'm Brady Soles. He's the anchor. I'm just a reporter. But the woman he's with is named Alicia Morgan."

"Oh. That's right." She smiled, but she seemed concerned now, as if Chandler had duped her into thinking he was someone other than himself. "Are you doing a story on the hospital?"

"What? Oh. No. I'm just visiting a friend."

She stared, waiting.

"Philip Jaco," he said. "Room two-forty-two."

"Of course. Mr. Jaco. Well, I'm glad someone's

finally come to see him. Poor man. His family never comes. Only the police."

"He's a loner," Chandler said. "Likes to keep to himself. Not many friends, you know."

"I see."

"I was just coming by to say hello," he said. He started to walk away. "This way?"

She nodded. "Just around the corner. But don't expect him to say hello back. He's not in good spirits. Some of his bandages come off Friday, if his doctor comes. These aren't visiting hours, you know."

Chandler nodded and moved quickly down the hall, counting room numbers. Then he peered into the semi-dark, private room, smelling the medicine and feeling the stillness. He walked cautiously toward the bed. Jaco seemed asleep.

"Mr. Jaco," Chandler whispered at the bandages. "Mr. Jaco."

There was no response. He moved closer.

"Mr. Jaco."

He stood still and listened. There was no sound. None at all.

Chandler suddenly leaned back. He began to walk backwards with his eyes locked on Jaco. Something was wrong.

"Nurse," he shouted. "Come here—quick!"

Chandler had by this time backed all the way into the hall. The nurse named Lisa ran toward him.

"What's wrong, Mr. Harris?"

Chandler stood with a stunned look in his eyes.

"Lisa, I just walked in and tried to speak to him...I didn't touch anything. Go look at him. Jaco—I think he's dead!"

The nurse walked to Jaco's bed and checked his vital signs. There were none. She pressed the call button and then picked up the phone and dialed for help. Quickly, other hospital personnel scurried into the room, checked for a pulse, listened for breath. A doctor walked in and pushed his way to Jaco. He felt his neck and then, noticing a bulge in the sheet, pulled it back to reveal a large needle-like object protruding from Jaco's chest.

"What the hell is this?"

The doctor turned, accusing.

"I'll call the police," said the nurse named Lisa.

"That won't be necessary," responded a voice in the doorway. Captain Montgomery walked slowly into the room. She looked briefly at Phil Jaco then turned immediately to Chandler Harris. "What the hell are you doing here?"

"I came to ask some questions."

"Who gave you permission?"

"Who needed to?"

Captain Montgomery turned to the doctor. "What happened here?"

"This." The doctor pointed to the small needle in Jaco's heart.

"How long's he been dead?"

"Minutes."

Her critical eyes returned to Chandler. "You found him?"

"I found him dead."

"You and who else?"

"Me and nobody. I came alone."

"You were here alone? And he's been dead for a few minutes. That's not good, Chandler. That's not good."

Chandler froze. For the first time, it occurred to him that either he had just missed the killer...or he *was* the killer, as far as Captain Montgomery was concerned. The thought infuriated him.

"If you're thinking what I think you're thinking," he said, "you're really in trouble on this case. I didn't kill Jaco, and you damn well know it."

As Montgomery watched, Chandler stormed out the door. He didn't speak to either of the young women who had eagerly greeted him a few moments before.

Perspiration beaded up on his forehead as Chandler raced back to the television station. Over and over, he asked himself if he were really a murder suspect, and if so, who had set him up—and how did they do it. It had to be someone who knew he was heading to Jaco's room. But no one knew that. Perhaps, he hoped, it was just a coincidence.

He parked beside the side door and rushed into the studio, saying nothing about what he had just witnessed. Alicia stopped him beside the anchor desk.

"What's wrong?"

"Nothing," Chandler said. "I'm just late. That's all. I'm fine. Are we ready?"

"We're ready," Alicia said, staring at him.

"Alicia," Chandler said, as she turned away.

"Yes?"

Chandler took a deep breath. He looked around the studio, then whispered to his co-anchor. "Phil Jaco was just murdered."

"What?"

"In the hospital. Somebody killed him."

"How do you know?"

"I was there. I just left there."

"You went to see him?"

"Yeah," Chandler said. "And he was dead. They think I did it."

"The police think you did it?"

"They walked right in behind me. I was alone in the room where Phil Jaco was just murdered. What would you think?"

"I'd think you're in trouble, that's what I'd think. Can you do the show?"

"Yeah. I'm okay. Let's do the show."

The call-in program opened with a report on Burke's funeral, re-cut from the previous day's news. While the tape rolled, the police officers on the volunteer desk watched solemnly, without comment. Two of the veteran call-in volunteers, Shawn and Dorothy, paced behind the police officers like school teachers watching their students. Dorothy, an older woman who came to the TV station dressed as a debutante, kept asking each officer if she could get him something—coffee, a Coke, a cup of water. Finally, two officers agreed to the water just to get Dorothy to leave them alone. Shawn was less obsessive, preferring to make small talk with the officers, offering his expertise on how to handle interesting calls. He had done it for years and had a skill for making sense of seemingly irrelevant information. Shawn was just a wisp of a human being, a short, skinny fellow with an uncharacteristic low voice which belied his physical appearance. Behind his horn-rimmed glasses, he resembled Buddy Holly, though he did not know it.

After the tape, Chandler and Alicia stood in front of the phone bank and restated the appeal for the public's help in solving the crime. It was like the invitation at the conclusion of a revival service, Chandler thought, with Chandler and Alicia urging sinners to come forward and confess.

Several callers responded, and the police said some of the calls were credible. Most were not. Maybe the coveted key witness wasn't watching television. Or maybe he didn't exist.

No one knew.

After they closed the show, Chandler and Alicia rushed to the anchor desk, where a production assistant had placed their scripts for them. Hurriedly, they looked over the first two or three pages, enough to help them get the show launched. They could examine the next two or three while in tape from a reporter.

Three miles away, Amos James sat in his toll booth, watching the credits for the call-in scroll on his portable TV. Twice, he picked up the phone but put it down without dialing.

Amos squirmed in the tiny cubical. By the time he mustered the nerve to make the call, the evening news had started. Maybe he'd mention it to Chandler the next time he crossed the bridge. Maybe. A car pulled up, and its driver handed Amos a quarter. It was a woman driver, with a baby asleep behind her, and after the car pulled beyond the toll gate, Amos picked up the phone and dialed the newsroom.

"4 News, may I help you?"

"This is Amos James. I want to speak to a police officer."

"I'm sorry, sir," said the intern. "The police officers are gone. Can someone else help you?"

"Give me Chandler Harris."

"Who may I say is calling, please?"

"I told you. Amos James."

"Please hold, Mr. James. I'll see if Mr. Harris is available."

"I know he's available. I just saw him!"

"Just a moment, sir."

The line went silent for a moment, and then the intern picked up the phone again.

"Sir," the intern said, sounding sheepish. "Mr. Harris is on the air. He can't talk now. May I take a message?"

Amos glanced at the TV set and saw Chandler Harris

reading the news.

"No," Amos said. "No message."

He hung up and waited for the news to be over. At 6:33, he dialed again. This time, the intern put him directly to Chandler's desk.

"Hello, Amos. This is Chandler. What's up?"

"You need better help. That kid that answered the phone, I didn't get along very well with him."

"You know kids. I'll speak to him about it. So what's up?"

"That guy you're looking for, the one who killed Officer Burke. I think I may have seen him."

"When?"

"Right after you went by—you know, Saturday morning—when the officer was shot. This car—some foreign sports car—it came tearing down the hill and ran the toll booth. I think he scraped the concrete barrier with his left fender. There was a car in front of him, so he backed up and went around to the other lane. That's when he scraped the concrete. Then he sped off. You know, like he was running from something."

"Did you get a license number?"

"No, he was going too fast. I think it was an out-of-state plate, though."

"Did you get a look at the driver?"

"Not really. I'm not even sure it was a man. If it was, he needed a hair cut. He had long black hair, and it wasn't neat. You see them all the time, those guys trying to act tough by looking like girls."

"Tell me more about the car."

"It was red. Bright red. A two-seater. I've never seen one like it."

"Did you notice anything else?"

"No. Just what I told you."

"Give me your number. I'm going to pass this onto Captain Montgomery, and she'll probably want to call you."

Chandler wrote down Amos's number and thanked him. Then he called Montgomery's office. She was out, so he left the information on her voice mail. He drove through a Wendy's drive-thru for a hamburger and, on an impulse, cruised past the Sunset Lounge. The parking lot was filled with cars. Its owner had been dead less than a week, but no one at the Sunset seemed to care. It apparently had been a very brief period of mourning.

He turned around and drove slowly back to the station, considering what Amos had told him. It made sense. Somebody who had shot a cop and beaten another man nearly to death would have reason to drive a little erratically. But why would the killer be heading across the Boulevard Bridge?

That was exactly the opposite direction of where he was heading when Burke was shot.

12

The next afternoon, Chandler sat at his desk idly, looking at the number for the Sunset Lounge. He felt certain that a killer moved along the same streets that he drove every day. The idea scared him some, but excited him more. His too-long delayed conversation with Phil Jaco was no longer possible, and he could no longer justify his earlier thought that Jaco's beating was not intended to be a homicide. Unless...unless something had changed that made it necessary to kill Jaco. He picked up the phone and dialed the Sunset Lounge.

The phone rang six times before someone picked up the receiver, listened to Chandler say hello and, without saying a word, hung up. That alone heightened his curiosity.

"Woody," Chandler called out. "I need to slip back out for a moment. Is that a problem?"

Woody shrugged. "We'll survive. It won't be easy, but we've been in tough places before. I'll page you if we need backup."

"Thanks, Woody. You're a good man. Sincere too."

Chandler hurried out the side door, removing his tie as he went. He rolled up his sleeves as he crossed the lot.

Five cars sat in the parking lot when Chandler pulled up in front of the Sunset Lounge, yet when he got out and tried the door, it was locked. He leaned his face between the bars over the door and tried to peer inside, but a faded shade blocked his view. Perhaps, he thought, they were having an invitations-only wake for the late owner.

He stepped back and looked around. A sign beside the door announced the imminent arrival of a Playmate named Patsy Peaks. He wondered if anyone would go to the trouble of calling Ms. Peaks to tell her not to bother. Chandler had never been this close to the building in broad daylight. It was more run-down than he'd expected. Darkness hides so many imperfections. Paint pealed from the one-story structure. Weeds reached up through cracks in the sidewalk. Flynn hadn't put much money back into his business, apparently, but Chandler supposed he wouldn't have either.

He knocked on the door. He waited, then knocked again. Moments passed before a woman lifted the shade. It was Mary Anne, the Sunset's manager. He remembered her. She was the one who wore clothes. Today, she wore a frumpy brown dress, and with her hair pulled back in an untidy ponytail, she didn't look like she was the sort to work in a topless bar. Despite her unkempt appearance, she wore entirely too much makeup. It looked as if Tammy Faye Bakker had found work. Unlike Tammy Faye, though, Mary Anne seemed to have intentionally made herself unattractive. She peeked at Chandler for a moment and opened the door a crack.

"My name's Chandler Harris, and I—"

"I know who you are. But we're closed. What do you want?"

"Can I talk to you?"

"What about?"

"I want to know who killed your boss."

She opened the door a little wider. "Why?"

"Because I'm a reporter, that's why."

"What about that cop who got shot? Why aren't you working on that?"

"I am working on that. Everybody's working on that. But I'm also working on Nick. May I come in?"

Mary Anne reluctantly stepped back.

"Thanks," Chandler said, stepping through the doorway and shutting it behind him.

The place was dark. It took a moment for his eyes to adjust. The room seemed larger than he remembered, and darker. It also smelled bad, much worse than his apartment. An old man sat at the bar, smoking a Lucky Strike and nursing a beer. As Chandler watched, he took a drag and studied his smoldering cigarette, as if it were communicating with him. Two other men—younger and better dressed—leaned intently over a table near the corner to Chandler's left. Their tiny table seemed just big enough for a couple of midgets to share a cocktail, but these men were not midgets. At the far end of the bar, a blond-haired woman wearing a g-string and a bikini top put warm beers into a cooler. A cigarette dangled from her lips, as if it were attached. She tossed her hair back and added more beers to the cooler. With each handful, she brushed her hair again, then allowed it to fall forward again. She looked up briefly at Chandler, found him of no interest and continued with the beers.

"Thanks for letting me in," he said.

Mary Anne shrugged and pointed at a table near the door. "Sit down, if you like."

Chandler sat in the chair across from her and pushed a few empty beer glasses aside. The ashtray, spilling over with lipstick-stained cigarette butts, he left alone.

"You want a beer?"

"No thanks," Chandler said. "I can only stay a minute."

"Well?"

"I'm sorry about your boss being killed."

"I'm not."

"You didn't like him?"

"Nobody liked him."

"Then why are you here?"

"A girl does what a girl has to do. So why are you here?"

"I want to know why Nick was killed."

"Probably because he was a son of a bitch."

"That's not a bad reason," Chandler admitted. "But hardly just cause in the eyes of the law. I'm sure Nick made a few enemies over the years. Can you think of one in particular who might be mad enough to kill him?"

She laughed. "Do you want them alphabetically?"

"That many, huh?"

"There's a few."

"Have the police asked you about them?"

"Someone came by," she said. "But they didn't seem too worried about it."

"I suppose they think it's a public service," he said.

"The cops would miss this place as much as anybody else if I shut it down."

"If you shut it down?"

She glanced at the bar but didn't speak.

"Who owns the Sunset now?"

"I do," she said. She smiled and took a cigarette from a pack of Marlboros and lit it. "It's mine, free and clear. With a little help from some friends, I took it from the son of a bitch. Or should I say, he gave it to me."

"You were in his will?"

"You could say that."

"You got rich when Nick died."

"You could say that too."

"That makes you a prime suspect, doesn't it?"

"You think I killed Nick? Look at me. Could I beat a man to death?"

"You could have had it done."

"I didn't have it done. I just waited for it to happen. Sooner or later, it had to happen."

"He must have been a wonderful fellow. How well did you know Phil Jaco?"

Mary Anne seemed startled, but she did not hesitate. "I never heard of him. What's his name again?"

"Jaco. He was beaten badly last weekend, Saturday,

with the same sort of weapon that killed Nick. He's dead now."

"Never heard of him, like I said."

"But he could have come in here. I mean, you don't know the names of all your regulars, do you?"

"I know most of them, but I don't know if the names they use at the Sunset are the same names they use at home with their wives, if you know what I mean."

"Did anything unusual happen this past weekend? Anybody show up looking angry?"

"Everybody shows up looking angry, then we put smiles on their faces. That's why they come. Our business is smiles—all smiles."

"What was it that made Nick such a popular guy?"

Mary Anne slipped another Marlboro from the pack, even though the one she had just lit was still burning in the ashtray.

"Did I mention he was a son of a bitch?"

"Yeah, I think you let that slip out. Anything else?"

"Let's see if I can explain it in terms an educated fellow like yourself would understand." She paused a moment, as if calling forth great wisdom. "Nick was about control." She blew a column of smoke over Chandler's head and squinted at him through the haze. "He either controlled you or he didn't deal with you. If the girls didn't do things his way, they were out of here. He would lend them money, then when they didn't pay, or couldn't, he would collect in the back room. There was one girl—did you ever meet Flossie?"

"No."

"I'm disappointed," she said. "You're not the observer I thought you were. Flossie's our star attraction."

"So what did Nick do to her?"

"Well, I don't know for sure, but I can tell you Flossie didn't like it."

"So why didn't she leave?"

"She couldn't. She'd been in trouble for shoplifting, and she made good money here, more than any of the other girls. She couldn't make that kind of money anywhere else. I mean, why earn five bucks an hour flipping burgers if you can tease men for fifty an hour? The problem was that Nick took most of it. Flossie brought in the bucks, and Nick would always figure a way to get most of them. But you guys helped her out a lot. That's the only reason I let you in."

"What are you talking about?"

"You know that consumer thing you do, the 4 News for You thing? You help people, and I appreciate that."

"And?"

"They helped Flossie."

"They what?"

"Without 4 News she might have jumped off a bridge or something. They got her some money at a time when she was really desperate. Nick said she owed him money and threatened to get it any way he could. Then you guys helped her, and it turned her life around."

"What the hell are you talking about? We don't hand out money."

"The hell you don't. I've heard about lots of people getting out of hard times because of 4 News."

"Yeah, *help*...but we don't hand out money!"

"Well, okay. I don't know exactly how it happened, but it did. Flossie had some problems, she came to me for advice, and I suggested she call 4 News. After that, things were okay."

"Tell me exactly what happened."

"Well, Flossie didn't want to call, so I called for her. Then I handed the phone to her and let her talk. I walked away so she wouldn't be afraid to talk. After a minute, she slammed down the phone, and I thought it was a bad idea. But then there was a phone call for her, and a couple of days later, this money came."

"How?"

"An envelope addressed to Flossie was left behind the bar. It had cash in it, I think. There was a note inside, saying someone wanted to help. I assumed it was the 4 News thing."

"How much money?"

"I don't know, exactly. It wasn't much. But the note said there would be more."

"You're lying to me."

"No, I'm not. Why should I?"

Chandler leaned back in his seat and glanced around the room. "I need to talk to Flossie. Where can I find her?"

"I don't know where she is right now," Mary Anne said.

"When does she come to work?"

"Whenever she wants to."

"Just like that?"

"Just like that."

"How about a phone number?"

Mary Anne stared at Chandler for a moment and then went into the office behind the bar and returned with a scrap of paper. "Be nice to her. She's a good kid."

"Don't worry." Chandler stood up and slipped Flossie's phone number into his pocket.

Mary Anne opened the door, and after he stepped through it, Chandler heard her lock the door behind him. He stood under the awning for a moment, letting his eyes adjust to the sunlight. Then, with his heart pounding, he walked to his car and drove back to the station to confront the person who had told him about the Sunset in the first place—his boss, Irv Rafferty.

13

Irv jumped when Chandler burst into his office.

"You got a minute, don't you, Irv?"

"What for? Your contract's not up is it?"

"No. I want to know about 4 News for You handing out cash to strippers."

Irv froze at his desk. Both of his eyes aimed directly at Chandler. "What are you talking about?"

"Somebody just told me a stripper at the Sunset's on our payroll."

"That's absurd."

"That's what I said."

Chandler sat down across from Irv and studied his face. He looked a little sweaty, but then, he always did.

"Who the hell told you, anyway?"

"The woman who owns the Sunset."

"Mary Anne?"

"Yeah," Chandler said, surprised. "How did you know she owns the Sunset?"

"I guessed," Irv said. "And she's lying. The station's not in the business of running a charity for the downtrodden. Or the unclothed. We help lots of people, but not that way. And don't go blabbing it to everybody

The Sunset Lounge

until you can prove otherwise. We've got another call-in scheduled for tomorrow night, and I don't want to hear this wild tale of yours again because somebody might just think it's true. Just worry about reading clearly tonight, and forget about trying to be the next Woodward and Bernstein. And stay the hell away from the Sunset. You've got a moral turpitude clause in your contract, understand?"

Chandler stood up. "Sure, Irv. Sure. But I will find out. You may not tell me, but I will find out."

Chandler walked to his desk and activated a message left on his phone.

"Chandler, this is Mary Anne. I talked with Flossie and she said she didn't want to talk to you. She said if you showed up at the Sunset again, she'd leave."

Quickly, Chandler turned the volume down.

"So do me a favor," the message continued, "and stay the hell away from here. Forget everything I said today, it was just a bunch of bull. I'm not kidding, Chandler. Turn it loose."

Chandler took the scrap paper out of his pocket and dialed the number Mary Anne had given him for Flossie. No answer. He sat a moment and then dialed Montgomery's number, but before it rang, Woody called everyone into the assignment meeting. Reluctantly, Chandler trudged into the meeting room. Although he disagreed with the lineup, he didn't say so, knowing that it would only drag out the meeting. When it was over, he was the first to leave the room. Before he'd sat down behind his desk, he'd already dialed Montgomery's number. After three rings, she picked up.

"Brenda, this is Chandler. Got a second?"

"Why? Have you found Jimmy Hoffa?"

"No, but I'm making progress with Burke's killer. Have pencil and paper ready."

She laughed. "Go on."

"This past Saturday, a stranger rode into town in a red sports car."

"A red sports car?"

"Yeah. Didn't you talk to Amos?"

"Amos?"

"Amos James, at the Boulevard Bridge. I left you a message to call him. You did call him, didn't you?"

"No, Chandler. I didn't."

"Why not?"

"He's a nice old man, but he's not likely to crack the case. Amos is always giving us tips, none of which ever amounts to anything. He's lonely, and I think he just wants to be part of something."

"You're wrong on this one."

"Anyway."

"Right. So this stranger was a hit man from out of town—Amos said he had an out-of-state plate—and he came here to rough up Phil Jaco. He was driving home when Officer Burke pulled him for parking out in the street...he had run to a phone booth to report the Jaco beating. He panicked, shot Burke, then raced toward the Boulevard Bridge. Why the bridge, you may ask. Go ahead—ask."

"Okay. I'll bite. Why the bridge?"

"Because the cop pulled him heading in one direction, and he figured the cops would look for him in that direction. So he turned around and went through Southside. And here's a news flash: the killer wasn't ready to leave town. He stayed over and beat Nick Flynn to death."

"Not bad for sheer imagination, but it's a meaningless theory with no evidence to support it. It also lacks something we call motive. You have nothing to tie these three unrelated cases together. No one heard a shot when Burke was killed, which suggests that the gun may have had a silencer on it. But if your hit man had a nine-millimeter equipped with a silencer, why didn't he use it on Flynn and Jaco instead of going to all the trouble of beating them up?"

"I don't know," Chandler admitted. "And I don't know why he'd be carrying lipstick either. Do you?"

"*Lipstick*? How do you know about that?"

"I have my sources. Look, I'm not saying I'm accounting for everything here, but I don't think you can either, no matter what you do. I mean, women aren't in the habit of committing murder with sap gloves, right?"

"None that I've met personally."

"Me either. So should we say that the lipstick *has* to have belonged to the killer or do we have a little flexibility here?"

"Sure, I'll be there in just a second," Brenda said. "What?"

"Sorry. We've got a meeting about to start. Look, I have to admit that we haven't tied the lipstick to the killer. It could have just been laying there in the gutter all along."

"*Lying* there."

"Lying there, laying there. Whatever. And now that I think about it, it's possible that whoever shot Burke beat Jaco. We'll see if there's any evidence to tie them together. Okay? Now, I've got to run. Have a nice day, Chandler."

Chandler listened to the line go dead and dropped the phone back into its cradle. The newsroom was heating up, with reporters returning from the field with tapes to edit. He watched the activity idly, from an anchorman's position. For him, things wouldn't heat up for another two hours, and even then, it would mostly be a matter of checking his hair and clearing his throat.

Indeed, the process was so undemanding that Chandler's mind wandered two hours later, as he read the words from the scrolling TelePrompTer. Why, he asked himself, had Flossie sent such a stern, unwarranted message for him to stay away from the Sunset? Or did she? Perhaps Mary Anne just said that. Did someone get to Mary Anne? What if Flossie was the killer?

In the back of his mind, Chandler heard a woman toss back to the studio. For a frozen moment, he stared blindly at the monitors behind the cameras. A woman with a Channel 4 microphone stood in front of a building Chandler didn't recognize. Although he'd read the script leading into the story, he couldn't begin to recall the subject now. Beside him, Alicia sat silent, leaving Chandler alone on television with a hundred-fifty thousand viewers. She could have helped him, but she chose instead to watch him sweat. After what seemed to him like a hundred years, he opened his mouth and asked the obligatory question.

"Tell me, Elaine, what's the mood down there?"

It was a gaffe that might have gone unnoticed were it not for two things. First, the reporter had just concluded her story by talking about the mood. And second, it was Marlo, not Elaine.

"Damn it!" Frank shouted in Chandler's ear piece. "It's Marlo, and we're already thirty seconds heavy. What the hell are you doing? Terminate this interview immediately."

"Thank you very much, Marlo," Chandler blurted.

On the monitors, he saw Marlo stop mid-sentence and stare at the camera for a fraction of a second. Then Chandler's face appeared, and before he began reading the next story, he briefly watched himself look unnerved.

"Speed it up," Frank growled.

"We'll have more news in a moment," Alicia said, finally, and the director cut to a commercial break. Immediately, Irv burst into the studio.

"What the hell's the matter with you?"

"I'm sorry," Chandler said. "I just zoned. It won't happen again."

"It damn well better not happen again." Irv stood for a moment, glaring at Chandler, then said what Chandler did not want to hear. "The newsroom is full of people who would like to anchor the news. If you can't do it, we'll find someone who can."

14

The other reporters teased Chandler about the gaffe the next day, and he kept a low profile until the 4 News call-in began at five o'clock. Only two representatives from the police department showed up. One of them was Brenda Montgomery. Officer Robinson apparently had something more pressing. Brenda and the other officer were carefully placed around the regular call-in volunteers to show up in every shot to give the program the punch it needed.

As they filed in and took their seats before air-time, Chandler studied the 4 News volunteers. One of them, according to Mary Anne, had talked to both her and Flossie. It seemed like an unlikely crew of suspects.

Dorothy Shaw, a petite woman in her sixties, had been there the longest. She always cuddled her phone and leaned away from the desk so that no one else could hear a conversation she considered private, no matter what its nature. He looked at Allison Figget, a retired English teacher who engaged each caller in lengthy conversation whether there was a need for it or not. Next to Allison sat Clyde, the grossly overweight and gregarious former engineer who leaned halfway across the desk and spoke so loudly that the other volunteers could hardly hear their own conversations. It was because of Clyde's booming voice that the 4 News phone bank had been moved to a remote corner of the studio, away from the anchors trying to read the news. And finally, at the end of the table, sat the mild-mannered Shawn Dibble, the forty-year-old computer consultant whose volunteer work at the station was exemplary. He was the youngest, the wealthiest and perhaps the most generous.

An unlikely lineup of suspects, indeed, Chandler thought, disappointed.

The floor director counted down the seconds before air-time, and Alicia and Chandler lifted their microphones and smiled at the cameras. Once the red light came on, Alicia went through the usual routine of urging someone to "break the code of silence" that had strangled the city, while Chandler stood beside her and nodded. The phones began to ring.

One caller refused to divulge his information to anyone but a police officer. Brenda agreed to take the call. After a few moments, she shook her head and hung up the phone. During the first break, Chandler walked over to her chair.

"What was that all about?"

"You don't want to know," she said.

"Come on."

She sighed and read from her notepad. "'Crime will continue unless a revival of the Spirit sweeps this evil city. If the police would set the example, everybody else would follow'."

The Sunset Lounge

"I think that's a great idea," Chandler said. "I've been worried about your spirit."

"Yeah. It needs some work. Good thing I bothered to show up, huh?"

Chandler shook his head and walked to the end of the volunteers' table and began quietly asking if any of the regular volunteers had taken a call from a topless dancer in trouble. Dorothy was shocked to hear the question.

"A stripper!" she exclaimed. "Heavens, no."

She seemed shaken by the question and hurried out of the studio to get a drink of water.

Allison said with an embarrassed but eager grin that most of her callers were not nearly so interesting, but if a stripper called, she'd let him know. Then she began to recite other calls Chandler might be interested in. He listened long enough to be polite.

Then he turned to Shawn. Shawn said he had never taken a call from a stripper either and added that he wished the calls he did take were as interesting. Shawn smiled brightly. Chandler wondered if Shawn had ever even had a date, let alone seen a woman take off her clothes.

Clyde, however, remembered the call, and, of course, he would have explained to everyone in the studio the pertinent details, had not Chandler hushed him up and asked him to meet him after the show.

The call-in effort did not improve noticeably as the evening wore on. Some callers insisted on a variety of alterations in society to correct the evils that beset it. Some called simply to take advantage of the opportunity to voice their opinions. Some spouted racial fears. Some called for an end to welfare. Most made no meaningful contribution to the investigation of Officer Burke's murder.

Twice during the evening, Chandler slipped back to his desk and dialed the Sunset. The first time, the phone simply rang and rang. On the second call, someone picked up but left him on hold so long he hung up. After the broadcast ended, he periodically wandered back to the studio to do a cut-in or simply hang around with the police officers, hoping one of them would drop a nugget of information.

During a lull, Brenda waved him over. "So, what's new on the anchor-detective beat?"

"You don't want to know."

"Sure I do, Chandler. Have you made any headway?"

"Not since we last talked. I think, Brenda, there's something here, and if you don't help me, I'll do it alone."

"We're working on it, Chandler. We're looking at everything to see if there is any connection at all between Burke and Jaco. I'll let you know."

"Hey, Chandler," Shawn called out from the far end of the table. "I've got one for you."

Chandler excused himself from Captain Montgomery and walked down the length of the table. "What have you got?"

"A caller made me promise I'd tell you that *justice will be done*."

"That's it?"

"Afraid so, buddy."

"Thanks, Shawn. It's a pleasant thought, I guess."

After the call-in ended, Chandler called Clyde out the back door of the studio, where no one else would hear them talk.

"Tell me more about that call from the stripper."

"I remember the call quite well," Clyde said. "She said some man had messed with her, and she wanted him to pay for what he did. So he wouldn't do it again."

"Wouldn't do what again?"

"She didn't say."

"So, what did you tell her?"

"I just listened mostly because when I tried to ask for more details she got real nervous and said it wasn't for her, that it was for a friend. She said her friend was a dancer who was afraid to call because she didn't want to identify herself."

"So?"

"So I said I couldn't do anything unless she let me talk to the person who needed my help. Then she put this other woman on the phone. She said her name was Flossie, and she needed help. Then she started crying. I started trying to calm her down and said I knew where she could get help. I have a good friend at Social Services who works with mentally disturbed people."

"You referred her to a state-employed shrink?"

"I gave her a name and a phone number of a counselor. I thought if it was some woman problem...you know, if she was pregnant or something, she might talk easier with another woman."

"So what happened then?"

"She didn't like what I said, I guess. She got real mad and said she wanted justice. Then she...like, changed personalities. She said she was a stripper at the Sunset Lounge and invited me to stop by and see her act. That's when I decided she was putting me on."

"And that was it?"

"Pretty much. It was strange. I mean, I talk to a lot of people. But this call...I felt like, in the space of five minutes, I had talked to three different people. And they were all crazy."

"Did you discuss this with anyone?"

"Never said a word. Our conversations in 4 News are supposed to be confidential, you know. I just jotted down the entry and went on to the next call."

"Thanks, Clyde. If she calls again, I'd be interested in knowing."

"Okay. But I don't think she will. I know the type."

"Thanks, Clyde."

"Hey. Chandler."

"Yeah?"

"You like to fish?"

"Fish?"

"Yeah. You like to fish?"

"No, not that I know of. Why?"

"Just wondering. I like to fish. I thought I'd take you out some time."

"It's a nice thought, Clyde. Thanks for the invitation.

But I don't like to fish...especially in the winter time. Perhaps next spring."

"Okay. Next spring. We'll go fishing."

"Good. Next spring. We'll fish."

Chandler treated himself to a sub and chips and sat at his desk for the next three hours, thinking about Flossie and trying to call the Sunset. If he hadn't believed Mary Anne before, he believed her now. Just before the late news, he tried the Sunset one last time, but still: no answer. The Sunset thrived on its walk-in business. It didn't take reservations and therefore had little interest in answering telephone calls.

He anchored the late news without mistakes, then drove home and lay wide awake in bed, considering his big week as an anchorman. It was over. Next week he would be a street reporter again, no longer under the scrutiny the anchor seat had brought.

He had no idea that the Saturday waiting just a few hours away would change his life forever.

15

In the early-dawn glow that filtered through her kitchen window, Mary Finnegan paced nervously, not sure what to do. A widow for the last ten years, she lived alone with her thoughts, leaving the house only to go to church or the grocery store. But her night had been restless, and now, watching the yard begin to glow pink, she wished she had called the TV station when Chandler was there.

But there was something about all those people on television asking for help that made her nervous. They might think her a silly old woman or they might say something on television about her. She didn't know what they might do. But she liked Chandler. He reminded her of her son.

Sighing, she crossed the room and picked up the phone. She hesitated one more time, then dialed a number. Charlie Gladstone answered.

"Good morning, Channel 4 News."

For a moment, she did not speak.

"Hello, this is Channel 4. May I help you?"

"Good morning. My name is Mrs. Finnegan. Is Mr. Harris there, please?"

"No ma'am. Mr. Harris does not work on the weekend. Actually, nobody works on weekends at this hour—except for me, of course. I'd be glad to give him a message, though, unless there's someone else who can help you."

"No...no, I want to talk to Mr. Harris. Are you sure he's not there?"

"No ma'am. I promise you, he's not here. I'm all you've got."

"I need to talk to Mr. Harris. It's important."

"I'll be glad to take your number."

Mrs. Finnegan considered. "Yes. Yes, that would be fine."

"Your number, ma'am?"

Mary Finnegan felt a rush of fear. She was alone in her house talking with a stranger, on the verge of giving out her private phone number. Quickly, without saying anything, she hung up the phone and sat down to catch her breath.

"Weirdo," Charlie mumbled to himself, as he hung up the phone. Then, since he had nothing else to do, he invested seventy-five cents of the station's money and hit *69. The automated operator responded with the last number called. Charlie jotted it down and reached for the criss-cross directory.

The phone beside Chandler's bed rang at 7:22.

"Hello?"

"Chandler, this is Charlie. I'm sorry to bother you so

early."

"You should be."

"But this might be important."

"What is it?"

"A Mrs. Finnegan called. She wants to talk to you."

"Who the hell is Mrs. Finnegan?"

"I don't know," Charlie said. "But I do know where she lives."

"Wonderful. Where?"

"She lives on Lockdale Lane."

Chandler sat straight up in bed. "What did she say?"

"Well, she just called and said she wanted to talk to you. She wouldn't tell me what she wanted. I said you'd be back Monday, but she wanted to talk to you today. When I told her I'd have you call her, she hung up without giving me her number."

"You traced her number?"

"Right. Then checked the criss-cross and there she was. M. Finnegan, 1636 Lockdale Lane. That's right up the street from where that guy was—"

"I know exactly where it is. Give me the number and don't say anything to anyone about it."

Chandler wrote down the number, hung up the phone and immediately picked it back up and dialed.

"Hello?"

"Mrs. Finnegan, this is Chandler Harris. Did you want to talk to me?"

"How did you get my number?"

"The station traced it for me. What can I do for you?"

"Traced it! You can do that?"

"Yes ma'am, anyone can do it."

"I didn't know that. I'll be careful from now on."

"Mrs. Finnegan, don't worry. I will give your number to no one. But I would like to talk to you."

"I would prefer not to discuss it over the phone. Would you...." Mrs. Finnegan hesitated. "Would you come to my house?"

"Mrs. Finnegan, does this have anything to do with Phil Jaco?"

"Yes, it does. But I don't want to talk on the phone anymore."

"I'll be there in thirty minutes. Will that be okay?"

"Yes. I'll watch for you. But don't come in one of those TV cars. And don't bring anyone with you and don't call the police...and don't bring a camera. Please don't bring a camera and please don't call the police."

"Mrs. Finnegan, I won't call the police and I won't bring a camera. There is nothing to worry about."

"I knew I could trust you. I'll wait for you at the patio door. Would you like coffee?"

"That would be wonderful, Mrs. Finnegan. I love coffee. I'll see you in a few minutes."

The sun burst through the trees when Chandler pulled into Mrs. Finnegan's driveway. Jaco's house sat only four houses away, but a line of sculptured shrubbery blocked the view. As he peered over the hedges, Mrs. Finnegan threw the patio door open and waved him inside.

"I don't understand why the station keeps that old man with the hair piece on the air," Mrs. Finnegan said, as she led Chandler into the kitchen.

The room was immaculate, but the appliances were outdated—quaint, almost—and Chandler sensed that the woman had lived by herself for years. His eyes fixed on a pop-up toaster, the kind Brady Soles probably gave his former wife for an anniversary present. There was also a Sunbeam liquidizer, with glass bowl. He hadn't seen one quite like it since he was a child. An oak table and two chairs occupied a corner. A Delft pitcher filled with spoons sat in the center of the table. Mrs. Finnegan pulled one of the chairs out and offered it to Chandler.

"I think they should get rid of him and keep you as the anchor," she said. "Do you take sugar in your coffee?"

"Two, please," Chandler said, sitting down.

"Alicia Morgan certainly is beautiful. She reminds me of my daughter. She lives in Atlanta now. But she's white, of course."

"Of course."

"Her husband is a stockbroker. They have three children, you know. My son James—you're so much like him. He's in Washington, working for a big law firm. My late husband was a lawyer. I guess it's in the genes."

Chandler was beginning to fear that his hostess might have gotten him out of bed for nothing more than idle conversation. Perhaps she was just lonely. He had been called often by elderly people wanting company. In fact,

The Sunset Lounge

most of his public speaking engagements, including those at church, were for senior citizens' groups.

"Mrs. Finnegan, you said you knew something about what happened to Philip Jaco."

Mrs. Finnegan looked away and took a deep but short breath. "Up the street, there's a woman, a friend of mine, who saw it all. I won't tell you who she is because she told me in confidence, but I believe that when a crime is committed and someone can help the police solve it, they have a responsibility to do so. Don't you agree?"

"Yes ma'am."

"I haven't said anything to anyone so far," the woman said. "I told her I wouldn't tell, and I haven't."

"Yes ma'am."

"Well, my friend said she was looking out the window, and a man was running up the street. You know, one of those joggers. He had a blue running suit on, and black gloves. She said she had never seen him before and that he looked kind of strange, with long hair and all. She said Mr. Jaco was standing near his mail box drinking a cup of coffee, and the man went straight up to Mr. Jaco and hit him in the face. Then he hit him again. She said when Mr. Jaco fell down, he turned over on his side and screamed. Then, she said, this man went up and kicked him in the stomach. Mr. Jaco just lay there like he was dead! Then the man who hurt him ran up the street toward my house. My friend called me and told me Mr. Jaco had been hurt and wondered if she should try to help."

"Did Mrs. Jaco see the attack?"

"I don't think so," Mrs. Finnegan said. "I don't know."

"What did you do then?"

"I started to call Mrs. Jaco, but..."

"Yes?"

"Well, I was confused. You see...I saw the man too, I think."

"But you can't see the Jaco house from here."

"No, I can't. But I saw the man—right there." She pointed out the window. "There was a car parked right in front of the Reynolds' house. A little red sports car. I saw a man in a blue running suit jump into the car and drive away. He didn't come from the Reynolds' house—they aren't even home. They're in the Bahamas for Christmas."

"Would you recognize him if you saw him again?"

"No." She rubbed her hands together nervously. "I don't know."

"Did you tell the police about the strange car?"

"No," she said. "I didn't. You see, at the time, I didn't know the man in the car had anything to do with Mr. Jaco. My friend called and said Mr. Jaco was hurt in his front yard, but she didn't tell about the man who hit him. I mean, she told me, but she didn't describe him. That was later. She called me during that 4 News for You show and told me all about what happened."

"So the first time she called you, it was to say that Jaco was hurt, and then she called you days later and explained how, and that's when you remembered the car?"

"That's right."

"I'm almost afraid to ask," Chandler said. "You didn't see the license plate, did you?"

"Now, Mr. Harris," she said, smiling. "I may be old and scared, but I'm no idiot. I had already written down the license number before he appeared."

"Before he appeared?"

"I told you the Reynolds weren't home, and that car did not belong in front of their house. I copied the number earlier in the morning, just in case something was missing from their house."

"Will you give me the number?"

"On one condition."

"I accept, but what is it?"

"You never, as long as you live, tell anybody where you got it."

"I promise."

She opened a kitchen drawer and pulled out a piece of paper with a license plate number written on it. Chandler took the paper and slipped it into his wallet.

"Thank you," he said. "And rest assured: no one will ever contact you about this."

"It doesn't matter, Mr. Harris. I would deny it to my grave."

She let him out the side door and waved as Chandler got into his car and backed out onto the street. To show her that he intended to keep his promise of anonymity, he drove down the street, away from Jaco's house, and drove a few blocks along back streets before driving back up to Cary Street.

Traffic was getting heavy, and he wove through the cars with his left hand while with his right he fumbled with his address book and changed gears at the same time. There was only one person who could help him trace the license on such short notice, and at one time, he'd known her number better than his own. But after the divorce was finalized, he'd made himself forget it, and he almost hit a minivan of Christmas shoppers trying to find it now. Even after divorce, it seemed, marriage could be dangerous. Finally, fumbling with his little black book, he found the number and managed to dial it on his cell phone.

"State Police."

"Sarah? Hey...this is Chandler. How are you?"

"I'm fine. But I'm not Sarah. She won't be back until Monday. May I help you?"

"This is Chandler Harris with Channel 4. I need to speak with Sarah Prichard. It's very important."

"I'm sure it is, Mr. Harris. I can connect you to her voice mail, if you'd like."

"Let me try something else. Would you be kind enough to call her at home and give her my phone number? I'd ask you to give me the number, but you wouldn't do that would you?"

"No, I wouldn't."

"Well, will you call her for me?"

"Why not? I've got nothing else to do. Give me your

number."

"Thanks. You're wonderful."

Chandler set the phone down on the seat beside him and accelerated around an old Ford. State police headquarters was only a few miles away, so he decided to drive there on the chance that Sarah agreed to help him. As he pulled into the parking lot, his phone rang.

"Is this the famous TV anchorman I've heard so much about?"

"Hello, Sarah. Thanks for calling me back. It's been a long time."

"Let's see: one year, eight months, two weeks and three days."

"You're kidding!"

"No, I'm not. It's a hobby of mine, counting time."

"Sarah, I need some help."

"I know that. Boy, do I know that."

"I need a name from a license tag."

"I'm not supposed to do that."

"I know, but will you?"

"What's in it for me?"

"The undying gratitude of an old friend who hopes you're still around when he finally grows up."

"Your battery's getting weak, Chandler."

"My what?"

"Your cell phone, you idiot. It's going fuzzy. Meet me at the office. I'll be there in fifteen minutes."

"I'm there now. I knew you'd come."

There was the sound of a muffled sigh and the phone went dead. He tossed it onto the floor and waited. Fifteen minutes later, Sarah drove into the parking lot, glanced at Chandler and motioned for him to follow her into the building. She looked even better than Chandler remembered, though her hair was shorter. They said nothing. In her office, she reached out for the number, and he handed her the small piece of paper.

"That's a Maryland tag," she said, surprised.

"Didn't I tell you that?"

"No, you didn't."

"Can you run it?"

"Of course. It's Christmas Eve, so why not break a few laws for your ex-husband? Sit down. It could take a few minutes."

Chandler took a seat and watched Sarah log-on and type out commands at a dizzying speed. She read the screen and hesitated. Then she banged a few keys and leaned back in her chair.

"Well?"

"Behind you, Chandler. On the printer."

He jumped up and ripped the paper from the printer before it had fully cycled. He looked at it, then at her.

"Joseph Langetta?"

"That's your guy," she said, reading the screen. "916 Kernwood Avenue, Baltimore. Do you need the zip code?"

"No, but I could use anything else you can dig up on him."

"What's this all about?"

Chandler hesitated a moment, considering.

"It is my belief," he finally said, "that Joseph Langetta killed Officer Bill Burke. I can't prove it, and it may be a wild goose chase, but I have two witnesses who saw his car speeding through Richmond on the morning Jaco was beaten."

"And you reported this to the police?"

"I tried."

"They weren't impressed?"

"I didn't have enough for them to get excited about it. Actually, I didn't have much of anything until an hour ago."

"So what do you intend to do?"

"I'm not sure. That depends on you."

"What do you mean?"

"What's your attitude toward me right now—I mean, what are the chances you will dig up a little more info for me? Like...more stuff on Mr. Langetta."

"I can't think of a thing I'd rather do on Christmas Eve than sit at a computer and dig up information on some schmuck in Baltimore."

"Sarah, I'll do anything."

"Take that back—quickly."

"I'll do *almost* anything."

"That's better. When do you need this stuff?"

"I'm driving to Baltimore right now. I'll call you when I get there."

"You're what?"

"I can't explain it. I've been looking for this guy for a week. Now it's dropped in my lap today, and I want to see it through. I owe you."

"I know that."

"Please try to understand."

She stared at him for a moment and shrugged. "No problem. Think of all the practice I've had."

"I'll call you soon," he said, standing up.

"Wait. Take my home number." She jotted the number on a paper, and he slipped it into his wallet. "Call me at home in exactly one hour. I should have the information then."

"I love you, Sarah. I really do."

"I know you do," she said, smiling. "But so what."

16

Chandler passed cars left and right, as if they were rungs on a ladder, and soon he pulled up at the Boulevard Bridge. Amos was not on duty, but as Chandler moved through the gate, he noticed red paint on the concrete post. On the other side of the bridge, he pulled onto the Interstate and headed north.

Traffic was heavy, but he was able to guide the Saab through the cars rather easily. He tried listening to the radio to keep him company, but the commercials got on his nerves. Why, he wondered, do car dealers insist on doing their own commercials? He snapped off the radio. He hadn't been in Baltimore in several years, and he supposed it had changed. He tried to remember street names and was surprised by how many he remembered. North of Fredericksburg, he checked the cell phone's battery and called Sarah.

"Sarah, it's me. I've—"

"Turn around," she said, before he could finish.

"What?"

"Langetta's bad news, Chandler. You don't want to find him."

"Hold on. We're getting static. Okay. What, now?"

"I talked to a friend of mine at Baltimore PD. He says Langetta's been up on murder charges more than once."

"So why's he wandering around Richmond?"

"I'm sorry, Chandler. You're fading out."

"I said, 'Why's he in Richmond, if he's up on murder charges?'"

"He always manages to walk for some reason. They can never get a conviction."

Chandler maneuvered around a trailer truck which lumbered along in the passing lane.

"Where does he work?"

"I don't know about work," Sarah said, "but he hangs out on the Block. You know—"

"Yeah. I know the Block. Great place to take your mother."

"What's that, again? Couldn't hear you."

"Nothing," Chandler said. "So I've hooked a live one, huh?"

"I'll say. Have you turned around yet?"

"Not yet. I'm in Manassas now. Should be in Baltimore in a little over an hour."

"What the hell are you planning to do when you get there—other than get killed?"

"I'm not quite sure, to be honest. I've got my recorder with me. Who knows—if we talk, he may implicate himself. Then I can return to Richmond with a taped confession. How's that for results? Hell, I've got to do something, even if it's stupid. You know that."

"But this time your behavior is going to cost you

more than a good wife. Promise me you'll call me from Baltimore. If you like, I can have a cop meet you. That might be a good idea."

"Thanks. But not just yet. A cop would only mess me up at this point."

"Right. You want to do that by yourself."

"I'll call you. I promise. If you don't hear from me by...say, dinner time, then call the cops."

"I'll suggest they drag the harbor. Oh no—wait."

"What?"

"Bill and I are going out to dinner tonight."

"Bill?"

"Yes. Bill. You sound surprised. Did you assume I would sit here the rest of my life pining for you?"

"I'm happy for you, Sarah. Really, I am."

"Sure. Anyway, if I don't answer, leave a message. I'll call you back."

"All right. Don't worry about me."

Chandler turned the phone off and set it down beside him. He was immediately jealous of Bill, though he knew it was a juvenile emotion. He had no right. He tried to convince himself of that. Still, knowing that Sarah was with someone else hurt him. His eyes watered as he remembered the good times he had done so much to destroy. I'm a jerk, he said to himself. I am really a jerk.

Traffic slowed down again, and he was glad to find he had to concentrate on the road. Just after noon, he entered Baltimore city limits and drove through the sparse streets of downtown. Then he turned onto the

Jones Falls Expressway and headed toward Towson. Kernwood Avenue wasn't far from Loyola College, halfway between the exclusive Guilford neighborhood and the seedy side of town through which York Road was a major corridor.

He drove through the city for half an hour, and then he pulled the car over to the side of the road and sat staring down Kernwood Avenue. It was a short street and narrow—wide enough to separate the turn-of-the-century row houses on either side and provide single-lane passage, but not much more than that. After a moment, Chandler pulled away from the curb and headed slowly down Kernwood Avenue. As he drove, he read house numbers. 902, 904, 906...

916 was like all the other row houses, except for its lack of attention. The tiny front yard was unkempt, the windows un-curtained. Chandler pulled into an empty space in front of 912 and turned off the engine. He watched a skinny cat slip out from under a car and slink across the road. After it disappeared under a porch, Chandler picked up his cell phone and dialed information.

"What city, please?"

"Baltimore," Chandler said, quietly. "I'd like the number of Joseph Langetta on Kernwood Avenue."

There was a pause while the operator searched her database.

"I'm sorry," she finally said. "There's no listing for a

Langetta at that address."

"Thank you."

Chandler set the phone down and glanced at the street behind him. No sports cars. And still no movement in the house. Lacking the nerve to walk up and knock on the front door, he decided to examine the alley behind the house. If there was a red car and if it had fender damage, he would know for certain that he had found his man. Slowly, he pulled away from the curb and drove to the end of the street, turned around and headed for the alley.

It only took a few seconds to identify the rear of 916, but the garage door was closed. Concerned about raising suspicion, Chandler drove out of the alley and turned back onto York Road. After debating what he should do next, he parked the car in front of the Aunt Sarah's Pancake House on the corner. Quickly, he ducked out of the car and took a booth that allowed him to watch Langetta's street.

"Merry Christmas."

Chandler looked up into the face of a pleasant if overweight waitress.

"Merry Christmas," he replied.

"What can I get you?"

Chandler glanced at a placard announcing a turkey special.

"I'd like one of those," he said.

"Sure, honey. Coffee?"

"Please."

While the waitress took his order back to the kitchen,

Chandler dialed Sarah. Surprisingly, she was home.

"Sarah—guess what?"

"You're not dead yet," she said.

"Well, yes. I can't argue with that. But you'll never guess where I am."

"I hope you're on the way back to Richmond, but somehow I doubt that."

"Nope. I'm at Aunt Sarah's."

"I didn't know you had an Aunt Sarah."

"I can see his street from where I'm sitting. It's a dump, by the way. He clearly has no consideration for his neighbors."

"Gee, Chandler. I'm surprised. Why don't you waltz into the place and help him tidy it up?"

"Well, I thought of that, but I'm not sure he's there."

"If he's not there, he won't answer the door."

"But he might be there."

"Then he can invite you in and kill you."

"I wouldn't like that."

"No, it's not a good way to spend Christmas. But what else were you going to do?"

"Don't worry. I'm not going to confront this guy unless I'm in a public place with lots of people around. Even if I could just confirm he's got a dented fender, I'd be happy."

"Dented fender?"

"The guy ran the toll booth on the Boulevard Bridge. Amos said he was in a red sports car and that he hit the concrete barrier and dented a fender."

"Okay, Chandler. You've got me interested now."

"Yeah, and my battery's fading. Listen, I'm going to eat my eggs and bacon or whatever I ordered, and keep an eye on our friend over here. I'll give you a ring later. What happened to Bill, by the way?"

"Working late."

"On Christmas Eve?"

"He's a cop."

"Oh. I should have known. I'll let you know when something happens."

"If you're able."

"I'll be fine. Good-bye, Sarah."

Chandler ate his turkey special, drank three more cups of coffee and drove back to the top of Kernwood. It was almost five o'clock. He sat in the car for an hour, watching the street. Then he checked his micro-cassette recorder, slipped it in his coat pocket and began to doze.

He straightened up as a green Buick turned onto Kernwood and headed toward him. The sun had gone down, leaving a dark street, but Chandler slumped down in his seat anyway. The car passed him and stopped in front of Langetta's house.

Five minutes later, a large man with a ponytail walked out of the house and climbed into the waiting car. Then the car pulled away from the curb, drove to the end of the block and turned back around to face Chandler. As the car drove past, it slowed down, and both men inside looked directly at Chandler.

Chandler briefly acknowledged their stares and then

looked down in his lap, as if he were reading something. After the Buick pulled onto Cold Spring Lane Street, Chandler drove to the end of the block, turned around and followed it to the corner at York. It turned right toward downtown. Several blocks later, the car pulled over to the side of the road. Chandler did as well, fifty yards behind it.

Almost immediately, the man with the ponytail emerged from the Buick and walked up to a closed car dealership. Except for the empty vehicles on the lot, the place was vacant. The Buick pulled away from the curb and disappeared into traffic. From where he was parked, Chandler watched the man with the ponytail approach a service bay. A red Lotus sat in it. The man leaned down and ran his hands over the right fender. Then he straightened up, took a key from his pocket and climbed into the car.

Damn, Chandler thought to himself. The evidence had already been puttied over and buffed away. Still, it was a damning gesture. Chandler considered phoning Sarah with the news, but before he could dial her number, the Lotus burst out of the parking lot and sped past him.

Surprised, Chandler pulled into traffic and hurried after the car. It was difficult to keep up, though, and Chandler almost lost the car when, two blocks short of reaching the Inner Harbor, the Lotus turned left and sped down the section of East Baltimore Street known as the Block. At the last possible moment, Chandler changed lanes and followed.

The Sunset Lounge

The Lotus turned into a dark alley just beyond the Two O'clock Club, but the alley was wide enough for only one vehicle. Chandler started to follow the Lotus but stopped. He couldn't see the other end of the alley. It might be a dead end. He couldn't tell. Daylight disappeared from the Block sooner than other places. What if he drove in and the man in the Lotus was waiting for him? There was no way he would drive into a dark, dead-end alley.

He backed out onto the street and found an empty space at the end of the block. By the time he walked back to the alley, the man driving the Lotus was gone. And he could see the Lotus, like an obedient dog, sitting empty and expectant halfway down the alley.

17

The man with the pony tail couldn't have gone far in so little time. Chances were, he was sitting in a bar somewhere on the Block. But which bar? They all looked depressingly the same. Each displayed pictures on the marquis or window suggesting the most beautiful girls in the world waited inside, eager to take off their clothes. And at each doorway stood a barker, trying to get men walking along the sidewalk to come inside before the show started. The show, of course, couldn't start because it never ended.

Chandler knew what to do: go in, sit down at the bar and resist any advances by seemingly friendly women who needed nothing more than a steady run of overpriced drinks and a credit card number to keep him company all night. A man does not sit alone long in the bars on the Block, even on Christmas Eve.

The first bar that offered itself was the Fantasy Club. "Merry Christmas" had been scribbled on the front window with what appeared to be shaving cream, but other than that, it seemed unimpressed with Christmas. Chandler walked in, sat at the bar and ordered a beer. It was a four-dollar beer, of course, but he expected it would last long enough for him to accomplish his purpose. As his eyes adjusted to the darkness, he turned on his bar stool, looking for the man with the pony tail. Moments later, a lady sat down beside him.

"Looking for some company?"

"Not really," Chandler said. He glanced at the woman. "I'm just having a beer. I'm leaving after this one."

Chandler guessed she was twenty-two or twenty-three. He wondered how such an attractive woman could come to this. After a moment, he spun his stool around to face her.

"Do you know a man named Joe Langetta?"

"Joe who?"

"Langetta," Chandler said. "He's a big guy with dark hair, keeps it combed straight back in a pony tail. He works on the Block somewhere."

"He doesn't work here," the woman said. "But I think I may have seen him. Buy me a drink and I'll see if I can think harder. I would really like to help you find him."

She put her hand on Chandler's thigh and leaned forward. Then she called to the bartender. "Billy, bring me a double—the usual."

"No," Chandler said, standing up. "I've got to go. Here, finish my beer. I've hardly touched it."

Without looking at the woman, he dropped a five-dollar bill on the counter and walked briskly out the door. His knowledge of the Block had saved him, for the moment. Bar ladies commonly order "a double," which meant Chandler would pay for two drinks in one, mostly Coke with a touch of alcohol. There is considerable profit in selling eight-dollar Cokes.

For the next two hours, Chandler went up and down East Baltimore Street, looking for Langetta. But no one resembling him appeared, and no one he asked admitted to knowing such a person. The crowds were thinning out, and even the drunks began wandering home. He ate a hot dog in Pollock Johnny's to soften the effect of several half-finished beers and stuck his head into two more half-empty clubs. Then he reached the end of the street where he had begun his search. Behind him, around the corner, he could see the outline of the Lotus. He wanted to search the car, but he would not be that foolish. It looked like the bait on a fish hook, daring him to walk alone down the dark alley.

Behind the Block sat several smaller clubs that addressed more perverse tastes. Chandler had hoped to find Langetta before reaching them, but he seemed to have few choices now. He could return to the alley and wait for the red Lotus to come out, but without his own car, he couldn't follow it. He could return to the row house on Kernwood Avenue and wait, but the idea of confronting Langetta on a dark street late at night didn't appeal to him. He could find a motel and get some sleep, admittedly an attractive alternative, but then he would be back where he had started.

Determined to eliminate all the possibilities, Chandler walked to the corner on the far side of the alley and stepped into a club called the Love Nest.

The Love Nest was little more than a deep, narrow room with a bar running along one wall. At the back end of the bar, near the restrooms, a corner stage featured naked girls gyrating to the rhythm, oblivious to the music. Between numbers, they would wander up and down the bar, seeking companionship among the handful of patrons. It was a small stage, and only one girl at a time performed. Near the rear edge of the stage, a man played drums while another squawked melodies on an alto saxophone. Neither seemed happy.

"Would you like to buy me a drink?"

Chandler looked at the woman who had sat down beside him. She was one of the dancers. She wore a furry red wrap across her bare shoulders, and its fluffy white trim was apparently intended to make her look like one of Santa's helpers. At least she left something to the imagination, Chandler thought.

"I'm waiting for someone," he said. "Sorry."

The woman shrugged and walked across the room to the stage.

"Hello," a different voice said behind Chandler, a moment later. "My name is Josie. Would you like to feel my breasts?"

"No, thank you," Chandler said, refusing even to turn around. He knew what he thought he needed to know about his hulking suitor by glancing at the mirror behind the bar. Like the other girl, she wore a Santa's helper wrap, with a matching micro-mini skirt, but she looked more like a linebacker stuffed into a woman's Halloween costume than anything else. "I was just about to leave."

Josie was not put off. "Now, you don't want to do that. The fun is just about to start."

"Not for me, it isn't," Chandler said.

He started to stand up, but the woman grabbed Chandler's hand and forced it under her tiny skirt. Chandler jumped up and tried to run, but the woman gripped him by the shoulder and pressed his right hand between her legs until it rested firmly against—his private parts.

"Hey!" Chandler screamed as he struggled to free himself. "Damn it, let me go!"

Chandler struggled violently, but the man who called himself Josie was much stronger, and with little effort, he pushed Chandler to the floor. No one else in the bar seemed to notice. The drummer looked off into space, while the alto sax player squeaked "What Now My Love."

"Don't worry, honey," the man said, with a lipstick-smeared smile. "I'm not going to do anything to you. Not yet."

Chandler stumbled to his feet and tried to walk toward the door, remembering, with every step, that Sarah had joked that he would end up in the harbor. For the first time, he knew she was probably dead right.

"Wait a minute," the man said, before Chandler reached the door. "You can't leave just yet. I think we have something in common. We met earlier today,

The Sunset Lounge

remember? I want to know, Mr. Harris, why you were watching my house this afternoon."

Chandler's heart seemed to stop as he looked at this man named Josie and realized that he had found Joe Langetta. What was worse, Joe Langetta had found him.

18

"I wasn't looking for you," Chandler said. "I used to live in Baltimore, on Kernwood Avenue. I came to town to visit a friend. I just wanted to drive by my old street."

"Bullshit!"

Langetta scowled, and Chandler watched the caked-on make-up crack across the man's nose. Then, as the cracks worked their way through his plucked eyebrows, Langetta smiled.

"Bartender, a bottle of your finest champagne for me and my friend, over there."

He pointed to a table in the corner and steered Chandler to it by the arm.

"That will be sixty dollars," the waitress said, setting a champagne bottle and two cloudy glasses on the table.

"Pay the woman, Mr. Harris," Langetta said.

Chandler looked at the waitress and pulled out a fifty and a ten.

"It's customary to tip," Langetta said.

Chandler dropped another ten-dollar bill onto the table. "How about a receipt," Chandler muttered, as the waitress collected the money and walked away.

"Oh," Langetta said. "Is this a business expense, Mr.

Harris?"

"You could say that. How did you know my name?"

Langetta laughed. "You were the only-out-of-state car staking out my house. I was curious, so I made a call. Would it surprise you to know that I have friends in Richmond?"

"It would surprise me to know you had friends at all."

Langetta smiled. "Touché. Now, how about telling me the truth?"

"All right, here's the truth," Chandler said. He fashioned a look of confidence, leaned across the tiny table and looked Josie directly in the eye. "I'm one of three people who know that you attacked Philip Jaco at his home in River Heights."

Langetta smiled, unmoved.

"The other two people talked to each other and told me about it," Chandler said. "I didn't actually see it. They're eyewitnesses, though, and they know I am in Baltimore trying to find out why you beat Phil Jaco."

He was lying, of course, but he wanted to give Langetta a reason to keep him alive. If he believed Chandler was his only way to find the other two witnesses, Langetta might consider doing that.

"My only interest in this case," Chandler said, "is finding out if the attack on Jaco is connected to a similar attack on a man who runs a bar in Richmond. Quite frankly, it doesn't bother me at all that they were beaten up. From what I've learned, they both deserved it. I was just curious as to why, and I took it upon myself to find out. Now I know who did it and wish I didn't. In fact, I'd like to forget the whole thing."

Langetta shook his head. "I'm afraid it's not that simple, Mr. Harris. You know too much to simply forget the whole thing. And at least one thing you just said is incorrect. I don't personally know any barkeepers in Richmond. And I have never attacked one. I generally get along with barkeepers."

Langetta poured a glass of champagne and offered it to Chandler. Chandler waved it off. He had intentionally not mentioned the Burke killing, thinking it might mean the difference of whether Langetta decided to release him. But why did he admit one assault and deny the other? It made no sense unless...unless they were unrelated. Maybe Montgomery and the other cops were right. Maybe his theory was downright wrong. Not that it mattered much right now.

"I'm afraid I'm going to tell you a few more things you don't want to know," Langetta said. "And these things are correct. Listen carefully. Believe everything I say and don't even consider ever breathing a word of it. Assuming you're fond of breathing. Do you understand?"

Chandler nodded.

"I did not personally know Mr. Jaco," Langetta said, sipping the champagne. "I was hired to do exactly what I did: beat the hell out of him. I don't even know who hired me or why. All I know is that the job paid three thousand dollars cash, and the money was sent to me in advance."

Langetta poured more champagne into his glass.

"Jaco was not my first assignment or my last. I will be in Richmond again. Who knows when? If — listen carefully, Mr. Harris — if I am ever contacted again by anyone from Richmond other than my secret employer, I will consider it absolutely necessary to make one more trip to Richmond and rip you apart. You will bleed and scream. You will beg me to stop until you are no longer capable of begging. You will curse the day you ever heard my name. And Mr. Harris, if I am not extremely careful, you will die. It's happened before."

Langetta shrugged, lifted his glass and emptied it in a single gulp. "That's about as simple as I can make it," he said.

Chandler looked around the room. For a brief moment, he considered smashing the champagne bottle across Langetta's face and running.

"Don't even try it," Langetta said. "You wouldn't — no. Wait."

Langetta stood up and walked over to the counter. With one eye on Chandler, he reached behind the bar and pulled out a worn cigar box.

"Open it," he said, setting the box in front of Chandler.

"What for?"

"The best reason in the world — because I said to. In that box is a chance for you to prove how brave you really are. I'm betting my life you don't have what it takes."

Chandler dragged the box across the table and slowly opened the lid. A nine-millimeter automatic pistol lay in the box, with a box of bullets next to it.

"What the hell is this? Do you want me to kill myself?"

"That's your choice, Mr. Harris. With that pistol, you can kill yourself—or you can kill me. You do want to kill me, don't you?"

Chandler hesitated, wondering if he could grab the gun and load it before Langetta could pull out another gun and kill him in self-defense.

"I'll walk you through it," Langetta said. "First, pick up the gun."

Chandler looked at the gun and then at Langetta. Carefully, he reached in and took the gun in his hand.

"Good," said Langetta. "Now prepare the weapon for the defining moment. Load the clip, please."

Chandler set the gun back down and began slowly putting cartridges in the clip. Langetta made no move that suggested he had another gun. Chandler imagined that he had reached the point where he could insert the clip and pull the trigger before Langetta could do anything. He slowly inserted the clip. Langetta didn't move. Then he cocked the pistol and jumped to his feet with the gun aimed at Langetta's chest.

"Aim right here," Langetta said calmly, putting his finger between his eyes. "I will be out of your life, and these folks"—he pointed to the bartender, three or four naked women and the band, which was breaking down for the night—"these folks will explain to the court how investigative reporter Chandler Harris pulled a gun and murdered one of their own in cold blood."

Chandler froze. Then, without lowering the gun, he began backing up toward the door. Langetta sat at the table, smiling, until Chandler reached behind him and placed his hand on the door.

"Chandler, darling, do you see the bartender? He intends to shoot you in about three seconds. You are, after all, an armed robber."

Chandler looked quickly toward the bar to see the bartender holding a shotgun aimed directly at him. Slowly, Chandler lowered his own gun, bent down and laid it on the floor. The bartender responded by lowering his gun.

"Very wise, Mr. Harris," Langetta said. "I think you may live another day, possibly two. But let me offer this advice: do not even consider turning my name in to the police because that will do nothing but get you killed. You see, Mr. Harris, I have an associate in Richmond who's even better than I am. I will give him your name tonight. You will not hear from him, if I don't hear from you. But he will always be there, just in case I have a problem. Do you understand?"

Chandler stood motionless and said nothing. Langetta shrugged and lifted the champagne bottle.

"Nearly empty," he said. "Are you sure you wouldn't like to come home with me tonight?"

"I'm sure," Chandler said.

"Well then," Langetta said. "Get the hell out of here, but drive carefully. The roads are very dangerous during the holidays, and you are tired and very likely to have an accident."

It was another threat, one for the road, but given what he'd already faced, it was one Chandler eagerly accepted. Without taking his eyes off Langetta, he pushed the door open and stepped out into the cold night air. He felt as if a rope were around his neck, and Langetta wanted him to run until it tightened and jerked him back.

Watching him through the glass, Langetta raised his champagne and smiled.

19

Chandler sprinted through the deserted streets, looking over his shoulder, fearful that Langetta would be in hot pursuit. He stumbled over a large piece of cardboard, under which a derelict had settled for the night. His heart skipped a beat as he recovered his balance and ran around the corner to his car. The man under the cardboard yelled angrily after him. Chandler kept running. His fingers shook as he tried to find the key hole on the driver's door. He scratched the paint. He had been careful since he bought the Saab not to scratch the paint, but within a few seconds he had destroyed the area around the key hole. Then he found the slot. Inside, he quickly locked the doors and slipped the key into the ignition, fearing, in the back of his mind, that the car might not start. It did.

He sped out of the deserted parking lot toward Interstate 95. There were few cars on the road, but every one which happened to be going his direction was suspect. He imagined it was Langetta, cruising up beside him with the window down and the nine-millimeter pistol pointed toward him.

Once he crossed back into Virginia, Chandler stopped

at a truck stop to fill up the gas tank. He went inside to pay for the gas and a cup of coffee and then, on the way out of the parking lot, he parked long enough to jump out and relieve himself. He dared not go to the restroom or the nearby clump of pine trees. Then he pulled back onto the Interstate and resumed the cat-and-mouse game with the cars around him.

He pulled up in front of his apartment at four a.m.

Inside, the answering machine blinked with two messages.

"Chandler, it's me," Sarah said, on the first message. "Call me as soon as you can—no matter what time it is."

Chandler stopped the tape and tried to dial Sarah's number three times, but his fingers kept hitting the wrong numbers on the cordless phone. When he finally punched the right number, she picked up on the first ring.

"Chandler?"

"Yeah, it's me." He slipped into an easy chair.

"Jesus, I'm glad you're home. Are you all right?"

"Yeah, I'm okay, I think. Or maybe not. I don't know."

"What happened, Chandler?"

"I found him," Chandler said, closing his eyes. "Or he found me. And—"

Chandler hesitated. It occurred to him that he might not be alone—that someone else might be in the apartment, listening to him.

"Chandler? Are you there?"

"I'm here," he said, standing up. "Everything's fine.

I met Langetta, we had a couple of drinks, and I left. It was scary at first, but he's okay. I don't exactly like his lifestyle, but hell—everybody's different."

"What do you mean, 'his lifestyle'?"

Chandler walked slowly around the apartment, turning on lights and opening closets. He didn't hear her question.

"Chandler?"

He was in the hallway, checking the linen closet. Nothing. Slowly, he opened the bedroom door.

"Chandler? Is somebody there with you?"

"No," Chandler said, peering into the empty bedroom. "I'm alone."

"Tell me what happened in Baltimore, really. It's okay. I'm alone too."

Chandler turned the light off and sat down on the bed.

"Langetta told me nothing I didn't suspect already," he finally said. "But he did know who I was."

"What?"

"He knew my name and everything."

"Maybe he ran a check on your license. Did he see you in your car?"

"Yes," Chandler said. "But I was parked too close to the other cars for him to see the license."

"Maybe he recognized your face from TV."

"I doubt he hung around long enough after beating Jaco to watch TV. Or—wait a minute! He could have noticed the city sticker on the windshield. It has that big monument thing on it, and he could have easily picked up on that."

"That would certainly get his attention," Sarah said. "Think about it. He's just committed a couple crimes in Richmond, and suddenly a car from Richmond turns up in his front yard with some guy sitting in it, doing nothing."

"But lots of people have Saabs. How does he tie that to me?"

"I don't know. But—oh, damn!"

"What?"

"It's—it's at the TV station!"

"How do you figure that?"

"Think, Chandler. Maybe he's got a contact in Richmond. You show up in front of his house, so he calls them and says, 'Hey, some guy in a red Saab is sitting in front of my house. What's going on?' And the guy in Richmond says, 'I don't have any idea,' unless...unless he does have some idea, and the only way he could know that is for him to know you well enough to know that you drive a Saab. That's something your viewers don't have. Only people you work with know that, right?"

"Mostly, yes."

"My God, Chandler. While you were watching him, he was watching you."

Chandler sat on the bed, trying to imagine which of his co-workers would consort with Langetta.

"Did you manage to record anything?"

Chandler's mind was blank for a second. Then he remembered the microcassette recorder in his pocket. "Jeez. Are you kidding me? I was lucky I remembered how to open the door to get out, I was so scared."

Sarah laughed softly. Chandler listened, remembering, in a flash, their better days.

"Does anyone know you called up Langetta's records?"

"I don't think so," Sarah said. "I mean, there are access records. But nobody but my supervisor would know, and he'd have to get into the computer to find out. And he's never done that before—not without a good reason. I'm not worried about that."

"I am. Whoever this is knows that you and I were married. They know you work at the state police. And it seems logical to me that anyone with any sense would put two and two together. I mean, how else would I come up with Langetta's address?"

"You could be right. It's no secret I'm a cop. I guess that means we may both turn up floating in the Baltimore Harbor. Thanks, Chandler, for one last opportunity to be together."

"Sarah, for the next week or so, be careful. Don't go anywhere alone."

"And stay away from you. You forgot that."

"Yeah, stay away from me...for your own safety."

"For my own safety."

"You said you had someone else."

"I do."

"Stay with him."

"I will."

"I'm sorry, Sarah. If there's anything I can do—"

"Chandler...Oh, forget it. I'll be fine. You're the one

who needs to watch out. I'd suggest going to the police, but I know you wouldn't do that."

"It's going to be lonely without you."

"I know what that is, Chandler. Good-bye."

He held the phone briefly, listening to the dial tone. Then he pressed his recorder to listen to the other message.

"Welcome home, Chandler," a muffled voice said. "I'll talk with you soon and...Merry Christmas."

20

Chandler woke up late the next morning—Christmas Day—and immediately broke into a sweat. He tried to go back to sleep but couldn't. Finally, he got up, took off the clothes he'd worn to Baltimore and showered. Then he made juice and coffee and sat on the balcony, watching the woods behind the apartment complex.

He thought about making breakfast but finally decided he wanted to be around people. So he got dressed and walked down to his car. He ate brunch in Morrison's Cafeteria, surrounded by various bingo and church groups celebrating the holiday. At a glance, he seemed to be the only person below retirement age, but the cafeteria's quiet, timeless warmth appealed to him. From the cafeteria speakers, "Joy to the World" filled the room. It felt good. Nothing bad could happen at Sunday brunch at Morrison's, while "Joy to the World" played.

"I go to bed with you every night," a woman said loudly behind him.

Startled, he turned to see an elderly lady in a red dress draped with little gold beads, giggling loudly as if she had created a joke he had never heard. Her husband stood beside her, decked out in a green sports jacket and red tie. It was their Christmas attire.

"Channel 9 is a part of our family," the man declared.

Chandler smiled and did not point out that he worked for Channel 4. It would only embarrass them. He thanked the couple, and after staying long enough to feel awkward, they retreated to their table. He lingered over a third cup of coffee and then drove home.

No one had left any messages on his answering machine.

He spent the rest of the day watching a bad print of *It's a Wonderful Life*, and when it was over, he called his mother in Florida and wished her a Merry Christmas. She returned the greeting and made him promise to come visit next year. Then he turned out the lights, and, as he forced himself to sleep, the phone rang.

Chandler fumbled with the bedside light and found the phone.

"Good news, Mr. Harris," a muffled voice said. "You report only good news. Go to church every Sunday and never speak to anyone at the Sunset again or you are one dead son of a bitch."

With that, the caller hung up. Chandler sat still. He thought he heard something outside his apartment. He put the phone back on the hook and slowly moved toward his pants hanging on the chair. The phone rang again, but before he could reach it, it stopped. It rang a third time, then went dead.

The Sunset Lounge

Quickly, Chandler hit *69 to trace the call. He was not surprised when the operator informed him the call could not be identified. Chandler moved slowly toward the kitchen, gathering a shirt and shoes as he went. A flash lit up the window, and a loud explosion rocked the building. Chandler fell against the counter, then ran to the window in time to see his Saab lying on its side in roaring flames.

Police and fire units arrived on the scene almost immediately. Every light in the apartment building snapped on. Residents gathered in small groups, clad in various assortments of nightgowns and hastily thrown together clothes. The fire was quickly extinguished, and the arson squad began probing the red hot-metal remains of the car. The deputy chief was the first with a diagnosis.

"This your car?"

"It was."

"Looks like some sort of incendiary device."

"Wonderful. Brilliant, chief. How'd you figure that out?"

Chandler shook his head and walked unsteadily back toward his apartment. He jumped when a firm hand grabbed his shoulder.

"Mr. Harris."

Chandler turned to see Patrolman Melano behind him.

"Mr. Harris, sorry about your car."

"What are you doing here?"

"I'm on duty. It sounded exciting. I thought I'd come."

"Who blew up my damn car?"

"That's not important."

"Why isn't it important?"

"Because you weren't in it."

Chandler took a deep breath and looked at the Sergeant. Melano had a point, and he knew it.

"What's going on, Melano? Who's trying to kill me?"

Melano stared back at Chandler, almost as if he wished he hadn't said anything.

"If they wanted to kill you, Chandler, they would have. For some reason, they want you alive...scared to death, but alive."

"Who are they?"

Melano shrugged. "The bad guys."

"Are you going to tell me what's going on or not?"

"I'm not sure what's going on, and I for damn sure ain't going to pass along any rumors. But I will tell you this: mind your own business. Read the news, quit trying to be a hero, and...did I say mind your own business?"

"Yeah. You said that."

"Now I have to fill out a report. Can I have the car's registration number, please?"

"That's it? You want my registration number?"

"Look, Chandler. I know something's going on, and I suspect you have stumbled onto it, whatever it is."

"I think so."

"And that's why you're in danger. You've tripped a wire."

"Enough of this. Who's the bad guy?"

"I don't know. Honestly, I don't know. All I know is that..." Melano hesitated. "All I know is that Burke was involved in some shady dealings, and he went too far."

"What kind of shady dealings?"

"You're going to get tired of this, but I don't know. I think it had something to do with a gambling operation. He made a case against a local businessman for taking kickbacks from bingo games, the case was air-tight, it went to court, it stayed air-tight, but the son of a bitch was found not guilty. Burke got real mad and got real personal and insisted on continuing his investigation. He started harassing the businessman, trying to scare him into confessing. The man got a restraining order against Burke, and he was busted. He lost rank. Then he took on his own police department."

"What did he do?"

"That's where I lose it again. Burke managed to make everybody mad. He wouldn't let it go. He began to look for stuff on other cops, you know, like he wanted to take someone else down with him. He was bitter and decided to share it with everybody."

"So then he pulled a car, and its driver blew his brains out?"

"No, it's not that simple. I can't make the car. If somebody wanted to waste him, I mean *intentionally*, that was a stupid way of doing it. I think he was killed for another reason, and I suspect the investigation into his death reflects something not otherwise known."

"I don't understand."

"Like, if for some reason, solving Burke's killing might implicate someone else...in something else. I just don't know."

"You think someone knows who killed him but is afraid to say."

"Yeah, something like that."

"So why are you telling me this?"

"So you'll know that what you see is not always what you get. I think somebody is trying to tell you to forget the Burke-Jaco cases and go back to work at the TV station...or else."

"Or else?"

"Or else die, Chandler."

"And what about you? Are you going to turn your head too?"

"No one's perfect, and I've done more than most."

"Such as?"

"Such as saving your ass. If you butt out of whatever this is, you'll be all right. If you don't pay attention to what I'm saying...have no doubt: the next time your car blows up, you'll be in it. Goodnight."

"Wait a minute. Who was the businessman?"

"It doesn't matter now. He's dead."

Melano turned and walked back to his car. The smoke from Chandler's car continued to billow. The crowd slowly returned to their apartments, as did Chandler.

Christmas was over.

Chandler returned to work Monday morning in a rented car, suspicious of everyone. A common "Good Morning" prompted analysis for possible undertones. But he found none. He cast inviting glances at co-workers, like a radar sending out a signal. None was returned. His mail box remained empty; the light on his phone dark. It was a slow news day. No major story demanded unusual attention.

A break in the killing of Officer Burke would be such a story, but only he had a clue, and he was not telling. After years of searching for a big scoop, he was in the untenable position of not reporting the one he had. He watched the clock, and tried in vain to lose himself in researching a story on soil conservation efforts in the county.

At four o'clock, the front desk receptionist called to say that a package had been dropped off in the lobby for Chandler. Nervously, he stood up and walked down the hall. It was a small, thick package, wrapped in a manila envelope and weighing about as much as a small magazine. *Letter bomb*, he thought. Chandler's name was written on the front, in block-print letters.

"Who dropped it off?"

"I went down the hall for a minute," the receptionist said. "And when I came back, it was sitting on my desk. That's all I know."

Holding it gingerly under his arm, he carried it to the

men's room, locked the door behind him and sat down. After staring at the envelope for a moment, he lifted the lightly sealed flap and peered inside. A stack of fifty-dollar bills looked back. He took them out and counted them. There were twenty—an even thousand dollars. At the bottom of the stack was a strip of paper bearing a brief order: "Deliver tonight to your favorite dancer at the Sunset."

"Flossie!" Chandler said, out loud.

A voice in the adjacent stall answered. It was Woody. "Who's Flossie—and can you fix me up with her?"

"Damn, Woody," Chandler said, his face flushed. "I thought I was alone."

"Oh. Sorry. But you shouldn't allow women in the men's room. It's against company policy."

Chandler replaced the money, licked the flap and re-sealed the envelope. So Flossie was indeed getting payments. And he knew whoever was doing it had decided to make him a part of it. But the story about them coming from the 4 News volunteers still didn't wash. A fleeting thought stirred his mind: he and Sarah had not raised the possibility that Mary Anne knew he drove a red Saab. She had seen him get in it and drive away from the Sunset. Perhaps his target was not at the station at all, but at the Sunset.

He walked back to the newsroom and waited for Woody to return from the men's room. Then he told Woody he had to leave the building for a few moments.

"Give my best to Flossie," Woody called after him.

The Sunset Lounge

Cars and pickup trucks filled the Sunset parking lot. A police cruiser sat idling at the Burger King across the street. When Chandler pulled into the lot, the cruiser pulled away and headed down the street. Chandler hesitated. He didn't want to confront Mary Anne or Flossy in a crowd. He wanted to be around people, but not these people. He turned around and drove back to the station. He would return nearer closing time. He watched various network feeds and chatted with Alicia while she sat at her desk, reading a book of meditations by Maya Angelou. Eventually, after watching the late news from his desk, he found he was the only person in the newsroom. Another hour passed. He pulled his coat on and left the building.

The Sunset was still crowded, but he could wait no longer. He parked at the Burger King and walked over to the Sunset. Mary Anne greeted him at the door.

"Come in, Chandler. Where have you been so long?"

He shrugged and looked around the smoky room. There was a dark-haired dancer on the stage, gyrating with her back turned to him.

"I was just getting ready to call you," she said.

"Why?"

She smiled.

"Make yourself comfortable," she said. "Over there."

She pointed to a corner table, and Chandler dutifully followed her to it. By the time they sat down, her demeanor had turned more serious.

"I tried to keep you out of this," she said. "I did, Chandler."

Chandler said nothing, waiting.

"Did you bring the money?"

He glared at her for a moment and then reached into his coat pocket and threw the envelope onto the table.

"Don't worry," she said, slipping the envelope into her lap without looking at it. "No one suspects you of anything. I got a call. He said you would bring the last payment to Flossie. He said there would be no more for Flossie."

"Who said?"

"He."

"Listen, Mary Anne. I'm not involved in any of this stuff, and you know it."

"You are now, Chandler. After all, you just delivered a thousand-dollar extortion payment. You're an accessory to a felony. I'm sorry."

"Yeah, me too. Who's the money from?"

"A guy who owes Flossie."

"Who?"

"I can't tell you that."

"Can you tell me that you killed Nick?"

Mary Anne laughed and lit a cigarette.

"You're the only one with a motive," Chandler continued.

"Motive?"

"Looks like an open-and-shut case to me. You had a hit man kill Nick so you could take over his place."

She tapped ash off the cigarette and shook her head.

"I would have gotten it anyway, sooner or later."

"What do you mean?"

"Nick was a gambler. He was always in debt, and I lent him money. A little at first. Then larger amounts."

"Where did you get it?"

"Some of it I took from him. He owed me more than he would ever admit, so I slipped some aside as time went on. He never even knew. The rest of it came from my house. When Mom died, I took out a second mortgage. It wasn't much, but it was enough to keep Nick alive a few more weeks, and enough to force him to guarantee the loan the only way he could—with the Sunset."

"Now I know you killed him."

She shrugged and nonchalantly eyed the bar. "It sure looks that way, but it's not true. I was simply betting that he would default on the loan and I'd get the place that way. I didn't expect he'd default the way he did."

"So who killed Nick?"

"Somebody."

"That's not very specific."

"No it's not." She blew a column of smoke over the table and eyed Chandler through the haze. "Be careful, Chandler, and do exactly what you're told. That was Nick's problem. He kept thinking he was in charge when he had already given up his choices."

"Have I done that?"

"I'm afraid so."

"Am I going to be killed?"

"That's up to you. Honestly, I don't know. Like you,

Chandler, I do what I'm told. Unlike you, I don't fight it. It's your decision."

Last call for drinks prompted a brief scurry at the bar, and Mary Anne stood up.

"If you'll excuse me, I have a business to run. By the way," she added, pointing to the other end of the bar. "That's Flossie."

Chandler glanced at the final group of hangers-on gathered around the dancer. He couldn't see the dancer's face, so he exchanged his table for one closer to the stage.

It was his first close look at the woman he had wondered so much about. She appeared more perfect than he had imagined: beautiful, naturally beautiful. Long black hair glided around her face as she moved. He went closer. Her skin was perfect, a natural bronze tint without blemish. Her perfectly sculptured body moved gracefully across the stage. Clearly, she was far to elegant for this place. Chandler was drawn to her, as were they all. He stood up, magnetized. He prepared to move toward the group which had come to worship. But before he took a step, a hand touched his shoulder. Startled, he swung around.

"You'd better come with me, Chandler. I've got to ask you a few questions."

"Me? Now? What's going on?"

"Now, Chandler. Now!"

From the stage, Flossie watched as her new admirer followed Captain Brenda Montgomery to a police cruiser parked outside.

"I see you don't think much of my advice to stay away from this place," Brenda said, as they walked toward her car.

"No," Chandler agreed, angrily. "I didn't. But that doesn't give you the right to arrest me."

"I'm not arresting you."

"Well, what the hell are you doing?"

A police officer Chandler did not know stepped out of the cruiser and opened the rear door. With a slight nod, he motioned for Chandler to get in. Brenda took the driver's seat.

"Chandler," she said, "I feel stupid, but I have to do this." She paused for a moment for him to say he understood, but he made no comment. "We received a tip that you were at the scene when Officer Burke was shot."

"I was at the scene shortly *after* he was shot, along with a lot of other people."

"That's not what I'm saying," she said. "Our source says that you shot Burke. He said that he saw you shoot him, then speed away in a red sports car. We don't believe it, of course, but—"

Chandler lurched forward. "Are you crazy? What in hell are you talking about?"

"Our source described your car in detail. He also described the shooting exactly as it happened. He knew some of the small details that the media did not report. That's what makes him credible."

"No, Brenda. That's not what makes him credible.

That's what makes him the killer. *Of course*, he knows that stuff—he did it. You know damn well I didn't kill Burke."

"Of course, we do, Chandler. But I have to do my job. And right now, my job is to investigate reports that give us reason to believe—my job is to ask you to explain exactly where you were when Burke was shot. Where were you?"

"I was about six blocks from there. I was leaving River Heights after going to the scene of that assault you guys don't care about. I was on my way to MCV, and I went to the scene when I got the call from the TV station."

"So you were in the area?"

"I've told you that. Think, Brenda. If I had done it, would I hang around the crime scene?"

"Bad habit you have, Chandler, hanging around crime scenes. You're still a suspect in the Jaco killing, you know that. And now this. You were conveniently present at two murder scenes. You seem to think that, because you're a big TV star, no one would suspect you of foul play."

"You are, Brenda, what we sometimes in the news business call 'full of crap'."

"Okay, Chandler. I've done my job. I had to ask you, and I did. I believe you. That's the end of it. But watch your step. If you had been me, you'd have done the same thing. Now take my advice this time, and stay the hell away from where you don't belong."

He sat for a moment, shaking his head. He considered spilling his guts about Langetta, about the money, about Flossie's connection. But he knew that if a police officer showed up at the Love Nest to talk to Langetta, his best interests would be in serious jeopardy. He needed protection, but he understood that the two police officers in the front seat could not provide it. So Chandler got out of the car and walked to his rental car. As he started the motor, he glared at Brenda. Then he sped recklessly out of the parking lot, daring her to give him a traffic citation.

She did not.

21

A cold front moved in overnight. By the time Chandler awoke and made coffee, sleet had begun to fall. He drove to the station with the wipers on, cursing the storm. Then he found he had been assigned a live remote from City Hall on the city's plans to clear streets if necessary. He did his duty, but his mind remained fixed on the mysterious woman called Flossie. As soon as he signed off from City Hall, Chandler drove directly to the Sunset.

The storm had an effect, and business was unusually slow. A few men in business suits leaned against the bar and watched a skinny dancer with a bad die-job gyrate on the stage. Chandler took a table near the back and caught Mary Anne's attention.

"Where's Flossie?"

"Later," she said. "How about dinner?"

"Do you cook here?"

"We try," she said. "How about a steak?"

"You're kidding."

"Medium?"

"Sure."

The steak came too quickly for medium. Chandler

tried to hack off a few chunks of the rubbery meat, but his only weapon was a dull, serrated steak knife. He found his teeth equally ineffective. He understood why the Sunset wasn't known for its food. Still, he made a show of chewing through it when Mary Anne walked by. He hid the remnants of what wouldn't go down under pieces of soggy Iceberg lettuce.

Three hours passed, with the crowd growing and a string of dancers each taking their turn on the stage, but still Flossie didn't show up. Chandler flagged Mary Anne again and asked if she was sure Flossie was coming.

"Don't worry, loverboy. She doesn't perform until prime time. You'll see."

At ten o'clock, the resident drummer at the Sunset rolled his snare, strobe lights pierced the semi-darkness, and Flossie pounced onto the stage in a flaming-red g-string and matching pasties. She glided up and down the bar, teasing and then drawing back from the men who reached out to her. She leaned against a pole, then wilted to the floor, bending her back till her long hair nearly touched her feet. Then she snapped upright and moved away from two men who had allowed themselves to lean too far onto the stage. They left dollar bills where she had been, hoping she would return to retrieve them.

"Not bad for a good Christian girl," Mary Anne said, slipping into the chair next to Chandler.

"Right."

"No," she said. "I mean it. She has a degree in New Testament Studies from some Christian college in Tennessee. She's the only born-again Christian I ever knew. Hell of a dancer too."

"I almost believe you. I'm going in for a closer look."

Chandler rose and walked to the edge of the stage, where he stood with the businessmen and blue-collar workers competing for Flossie's attention. Abruptly, Flossie leaned over and spoke to him.

"You don't belong here," she whispered. "Or do you?"

He shrugged, smiling. "Where did you go to college?"

"Carson Baptist in Tennessee. But hey, everybody makes mistakes. Would you like to contribute to my graduate work?"

"I already have."

Flossie smiled down at him and then flung herself around and bobbed and weaved toward the other end of the bar. Chandler waited, but she did not return to where he was standing, so he went back to the table with Mary Anne.

"I want to know everything about her, Mary Anne."

"I'll speak to her, Chandler, if that's you want."

"I do."

Mary Anne left the table and disappeared into the rear of the Sunset. Chandler watched Flossie finish her routine. Ten minutes passed. Other girls took the stage.

Most of the men who had been panting at the stage returned to nursing their beers. Chandler took a last sip from his beer and had stood up to leave when he saw Flossie, nude to the waist, crossing the room toward him. As she sat down across from him, he extended his hand.

Brady Soles stepped into the cold air outside the newsroom side door, put a cigarette in his mouth and flipped his lighter. As the flame kissed the tip of the tobacco, a large man stepped out of the shadows and with one hard, well-placed swing embedded the burning lighter and cigarette in Brady's mouth. Brady crumpled into the snow and lay stunned against the building. Blood gurgled from his mouth as he struggled to get up. The assailant admired his handiwork for a moment, then disappeared around the corner of the building.

Brady staggered to his feet, pressed his electronic key card against the door and fell into the newsroom. Several employees, who under normal circumstances avoided the senior anchorman, attended him as if they cared. He was cleaned up as much as possible with warm, wet paper towels. Someone dialed 911, and a white ambulance rumbled toward Channel 4 to rescue the disabled anchorman.

"My name's Chandler Harris—"

"I know who you are," Flossie said curtly, ignoring his extended hand.

"I almost went to Carson," he said. "But Marshall University was cheaper."

"You made the right decision."

He smiled. "I've made a lot of bum decisions since then."

"I'm impressed."

"*Flossie*. What's your real name?"

"Flossie. That's my name."

"That's not what your mother named you."

"A lot has changed since then."

"Flossie, who killed Nick?"

"Beats me."

"Who killed Officer Burke?"

"How should I know?"

"How about Phil Jaco?"

"What's he got to do with this?"

"Then you know him?"

"Yeah, I know him. I used to work for him." She reached for a cigarette left on the table by Mary Anne. "The bastard works for me now."

"Oh?"

"Yeah. He sends me a regular paycheck."

"What do you do for the paycheck, if I may ask?"

"Don't worry, it's not what you think. Simply put, I let him live."

"*Did* let him live."

"Whatever. But if you think about it, if he were dead, he couldn't do anybody any good, could he?"

"He is dead."

"You're kidding?"

"No, I'm not. The money I brought last night is your last payment."

She, for the first time, looked intently into Chandler's eyes. "Oh well. So it goes. It couldn't happen to a nicer guy."

Chandler's beeper buzzed on his hip.

"Wait a second."

He unhooked the beeper and watched a brief message crawl across the screen: "Call Lindi immediately." Lindi was the eleven p.m. producer. At this hour, she would normally page an on-call photographer or reporter. Perhaps dialing Chandler's number was a mistake. He cleared the beeper and hooked it back onto his belt.

"I think Burke and Jaco are connected," he said. "But the only person who can confirm that idea threatened to kill me. So far, you haven't done that. I want to know who's killing whom, but I want to learn it from you."

"I don't know anything about that. All I know about is Jaco—the late Jaco, assuming what you said is true."

"Will you tell me about Jaco?"

"Why? So you can put it on television?"

"No, not on television. It's not that at all."

His beeper buzzed again and he lifted it to the light. Across the tiny screen ran three words: "Now Chandler Now!"

"Damn it."

"What?"

"I've got to make a phone call," Chandler said.

"Use the one in Mary Anne's office," Flossie said,

nodding at the door behind the bar.

"Thanks."

"Don't keep me waiting," she said. "I'm a moody person."

"I'll be right back."

Chandler stepped into the office. Lindi answered on the first ring.

"Chandler, we need you to come to the station immediately. Brady can't do the news tonight."

"What's wrong with Brady?"

"I'm not sure. Irv told me to get you to do the news. He said Brady had hurt himself and for me to call you. When will you be here?"

"Ten minutes."

"No longer."

"I'm on my way."

Chandler returned to Flossie and announced that he had to leave.

"Something's happened to Brady, and I've got to anchor the late news. I don't want to go. I want to stay with you, but I have to. I'll be back before midnight. Will you wait?"

"I'll be here," she said. "But I can't talk to you then. Maybe another time, Mr. Harris."

She smashed out her cigarette and rose to leave. Chandler reached out and touched her hand. She hesitated for a moment. Then she strode into Mary Anne's office and closed the door.

When Chandler arrived at the station, a police cruiser pulled out of the driveway. It paused briefly as he passed, then turned onto Midlothian Turnpike. Chandler parked against the fence and brushed by several people talking in the parking lot. Snow had begun to fall with the sleet. Inside, Chandler stopped at Lindi's desk.

"We'll talk later," she said, waving him off. "Here's the rundown and scripts. I'll bring the kicker in later. You've got three minutes. Comb your hair."

"Uh, Lindi?"

Chandler turned and saw Charlie standing up behind the assignment desk. He was cradling a phone against his shoulder.

"What?"

"It's Channel 9," Charlie said. "They want to know what happened to Brady."

"How do they know anything happened to Brady?"

"I don't know," Charlie said. "They just called and asked."

"Was it on the scanner?"

"I didn't hear it."

"Damn it," Lindi yelled. "Tell them you haven't heard anything about it."

She spun around in her chair, with her back to Chandler. Out of the corner of his eye, Chandler spotted Dave, the director, rushing toward the studio with scripts in his arms. Chandler ran after him.

"What happened?"

"Somebody punched Brady in the kisser."

"Damn," Chandler said.

Dave smiled and gave Chandler a thumbs-up sign as he disappeared behind the console. Dave had never favored Brady, and even though he had no idea who hit him, he was amused by it. Chandler crossed the room and settled into the anchor chair beside Alicia. Using her mirror, he checked his tie and hair. Moments later, they were on the air.

During the first commercial break, Alicia whispered the news to Chandler. "Brady stepped outside to smoke a cigarette, and somebody hit him in the face. That's all I know. Lindi called an ambulance, but Irv picked him up and took him to the hospital."

"Is he hurt bad?"

"I don't know. I don't think so. But he's missing a couple of teeth, and his lip was bleeding. That's what Lindi said."

"Who did it?"

"Who knows."

"Stand by!"

After the news, Chandler found Irv in the newsroom. "What the hell's going on?"

Irv frowned and pulled him outside.

"I need a cigarette," Irv said.

Chandler watched him strike a match and cup it against the wind. The snow was falling heavier now.

"You'll have to fill in for Brady the rest of the week."

"No problem," Chandler said. "So who hit him?"

"Nobody knows. He doesn't know. He didn't even

see the guy."

"Somebody walked up and hit him in the face and he saw nothing?"

"That's what he said."

"I don't believe that, and neither do you."

"It's cold out here," Irv said. "I'll see you tomorrow."

He crushed the cigarette in the snow and walked back inside without looking at Chandler. For a moment, Chandler watched the snow falling through the parking lot lights. Then he crossed the lot and climbed into his car and headed back to the Sunset. But he was too late.

"Sorry," Mary Anne said, behind the bar. "She's gone."

"Where?"

"Home, I guess. She said she had a headache and left early. By the way, I caught part of your act tonight. You're not a bad anchorman. I wouldn't be surprised if you got Brady's job."

"At this rate, he may have no choice. You know, somebody punched Brady tonight. Would you happen to know who did it?"

"I was here."

"Right."

"Good night, Chandler."

By the time he had pulled back onto the road, big yellow trucks were cruising up and down the Turnpike with their plows raised and a spray of salt and sand shooting across the road behind them. Chandler followed one of them back to his apartment complex and parked near the entrance, just in case the lot got snowed in.

It took him several minutes to navigate the ice, and by the time he slipped the key into his front door, he was so hot and tired with the exertion that he almost didn't notice how the door swung open freely, without his turning the key.

22

The apartment greeted him dark and silent. The air seemed strange. Something was wrong. He stood in the doorway for a moment, listening, and then he turned on the overhead hall light.

"Okay," he said loudly. "Who's here?"

"It's all right," a voice said, from the corner of the living room. "It's just me."

The voice was that of Flossie. She had gotten in—he didn't care how—and was sitting on the floor with her legs tucked beneath her. In the dim light, she seemed almost childlike.

"You should have been a burglar," Chandler said, smiling.

He tossed his coat on the chair and crossed the room.

"Are you a burglar or can I fix you a drink? I mean, if you're a burglar, you'll probably want to leave right away. If not...I'd like you to stay."

"How about coffee?"

"Sounds good."

He started for the kitchen, but Flossie jumped up.

"I'll do it," she said.

She turned on the kitchen light and began to rummage through his refrigerator.

"Hey—you've got eggs. Let's have breakfast. I haven't eaten today."

"I've got eggs? I didn't know that. Breakfast it is. Here, I'll help."

Flossie found a hand towel, draped it around her waist like an apron and turned on the stove. Chandler started the coffee, and the two buzzed about the kitchen as if it were a party. He watched her without being obvious, marveling that she had, only a few hours earlier, been dancing nude before a room of strangers. They ate the food standing up at the kitchen counter, saying little. Afterwards, he retrieved some logs from the balcony and started a fire.

Outside, the yellow trucks moved up and down Midlothian Turnpike in droning columns, but nothing moved around the apartments. The silence was reassuring. If the trucks did not come into the complex, it was not likely anyone else would.

"When I was a little girl, we didn't stay up late like this."

She smiled. The fire made her face glow.

"Dad always said it was the time for good Christians to get their rest, so they could be prepared for the next day. He didn't know much about what went on at night, but he was sure it wasn't good for anybody."

"He was probably right," Chandler said.

"I know he was, but it wasn't easy. We lived on a

farm, and we had to be up at four-thirty to milk the cows. I used to think they'd still be there at six or seven. But it was understood that four-thirty was the time to get them, and that's what we did. Nobody had an alarm clock. We just got up, automatically."

"I hadn't figured you for a country girl. But I'm glad you were."

"Why?"

"Because it makes me feel good about you. It means you haven't always been…I'm sorry. I shouldn't have—"

"Don't worry about it. Dad would say all things happen for a reason."

"I think he's right there too."

She shrugged. "Maybe."

"Let me guess: he believed that everything that happened—good or bad—was God's will. Like when it was hot and dry and the fields were burning up, he would pray for rain, right?"

"Wow," she said, smiling. "That's exactly what he'd do."

"Like I said, I know what you're talking about."

"No, I mean it. That's exactly what he'd do." She seemed excited that Chandler understood what she said. It was if, at least on that level, they knew each other. "Sometimes the rain would come, and he would thank God for the rain. He said his prayers had been answered. And when it didn't rain, he said that was God's will too. God couldn't lose. Whatever happened, Dad gave him the credit. Even when my brother

Michael was killed in Iraq."

"I'm sorry."

"Before he died, we worried that it might happen. We prayed for him every day. But there was no doubt in Dad's mind: Michael died because God wanted him to."

"I was raised in the faith too," Chandler said. "I don't see it the way I did as a child, but it's something that one never completely loses. Not completely, Flossie. Not completely."

Her face tensed up, and she walked across the floor with her arms folded across her chest. With her back to Chandler, she took a deep breath.

"My name is Martha Carpenter."

"I'm glad to meet you, Martha. I'm really glad to meet you. But tell me...Martha. Tell me about Flossie."

She walked to the balcony door and looked at the snow. "Okay. I wanted to me a missionary. I wanted that more than anything in the world. And Richmond is the East Coast headquarters of the World Mission Agency. I guess you know that."

"Yeah. I know."

"They said they had no openings, but I could stay in touch, if I wanted to. I asked for anything—a secretary's job, you name it. Then they got downright irritated and said I should just leave. And that's when I met Phil Jaco."

Chandler sat up and stared at her.

"He seemed to be my salvation," she said. "If you'll excuse the term. I had gone to a temp agency, looking for work. They sent me to an interview at Family

Bakeries. I got a job in the office, doing routine paper shuffling. Phil Jaco saw me and decided right there and then I had a bright future with his company."

"It's beginning to make sense," Chandler said. "But is that what made you lose our religion?"

Flossie smiled bitterly. "Can we have coffee?"

"Sure."

Chandler walked into the kitchen and fumbled with the coffee maker. Flossie continued to talk.

"Jaco called me into his office and said he needed someone who could work in the newly created public relations department. Of course, I accepted the promotion. When he almost immediately arranged for me to attend a trade show in Atlanta with him, it didn't dawn on me that he had something else in mind. But before I knew it, I was in Atlanta fighting off Jaco and some guy he called Leonard."

"Where did Leonard come from?"

"I'll get to that in a minute. At the time, I thought he was a business associate of Jaco's. Anyway, as soon as we got to the hotel, Jaco checked us into the same room, and before I'd even set my suitcase down, he forced me to undress and...and he came on to me right there. He tore at me, threw me on the bed...and raped me, right there. It scared me so much, I threw up, right on the bedspread. I was a virgin. I was a virgin and Phil Jaco took it away, just like that. I tried to get out of the room, but he grabbed me and threw me down on the bed again and said if I did anything he didn't like, he'd see to it that I disappeared in Atlanta, and nobody would ever hear from me again. I didn't know if he was bluffing or not. I was twenty-one, for God's sake, and scared out of my wits. He said if I ever told the police what he had done, he would say that I'd done everything willingly. He said the evidence would show that there never was but one hotel room, and I knew that when we left. He had it all figured out. But the worst was still to come."

Chandler poured a cup of coffee and handed it to her. His hand trembled. She took it without seeming to notice and walked back into the living room.

"Jaco said he was meeting friends for dinner, and that I was to go along with whatever they wanted to do. 'They' turned out to be Leonard. When we got back to the hotel, we stopped by Leonard's room for a drink. Jaco excused himself, and...Leonard did it too...he raped me. I screamed, and he slapped me. Hard. In a little while, Jaco returned, and he and his friend Leonard talked about how it would be their word against mine, and the best thing for me to do was relax and enjoy the weekend. They laughed and tried to get me to laugh with them, as if it was nothing."

Chandler set his hand on Flossie's shoulder, but she brushed it away and walked back to the balcony door.

"When I got back from Atlanta," she said, "I went directly to the World Mission Agency, looking for help. It was the only place where I knew anybody, and I thought they would help me. But while I was sitting in the lobby, waiting for someone to talk to, Leonard walked into the building like he owned the place. I screamed at him. I called for help. He turned around and acted like he had never seen me before. He said his name was Ralph Adkins. Some Agency types apologized to Leonard and led me to the chapel for counseling."

"And he's still there, isn't he?"

She started to speak, but her voice cracked and she simply nodded. Tears swelled on her cheek. After a moment, she wiped violently at her eyes.

"He's still there," she said. "Still leading his department in prayer every morning, filling in for vacationing preachers on Sunday morning. And the people who work with him think I'm crazy."

Without speaking, Chandler held out his arms and closed them around her shoulders. For a moment, she cried with her face buried against his chest. Then she pulled away and wiped her eyes again. The fire was dying, and the embers reflecting off her face gave it a warm glow. They stood close to each other, not speaking. Then Flossie took a deep breath and curled up on the rug in front of the fireplace. For a few moments, she lay there, motionless, as if exhausted. Chandler grabbed a pillow from the sofa and put it under her head. Slowly, he lay down beside her. The clock on the mantle chimed three.

Within moments, they were asleep.

When morning came, the snow was still falling. Except for a few four-wheel-drive vehicles, nothing moved on the streets. Chandler stirred first and went to the kitchen to put on a pot of coffee. The aroma woke Flossie. She walked into the kitchen, gave him a quick but serious hug, then wandered toward the bathroom. A moment later, he heard the shower running. He knew that there were no fresh towels in the bathroom, and that embarrassed him, so he found some in the closet and laid them on the edge of the bathroom sink. He hesitated for a moment, watching the magnificent form behind the shower curtain, then he went to the kitchen.

He rummaged though the refrigerator, found enough eggs and bacon to make another breakfast, then set the table and waited for his guest to return. He worried briefly about the meal. The eggs and bacon had apparently been holed up in his refrigerator for a long time. Martha came in wearing his bathrobe with a towel wrapped around her head.

"Do you want to toss your clothes in the washer?"

"Do you mind?"

"Go ahead. I don't think we're going anywhere for a while."

She started the wash, then sat down to eat. They exchanged small talk. He asked no more questions about the terrible weekend in Atlanta. She offered no more answers. After breakfast, he took a shower, and when he came out, Flossie stood looking out the window at a group of kids sledding down the hills beyond the parking lot.

"You don't have a sled, do you?"

"No," he said. "That's one thing I never got around

to. I was hoping Santa Claus would drop one off, but he skipped my place this year, once again. But you came. Are you from Santa Claus, Martha?"

She smiled. "Let's go over there and see if they will let us borrow one of their sleds."

"Will you be warm enough? I mean, your hair isn't even dry yet."

"I'll dry it. Where's your dryer? You TV types have hair dryers, don't you?"

"You won't believe this, but I don't use a hair dryer. I do, however, happen to have one—just for emergencies like this."

He retrieved a hair dryer from under the bathroom sink and then dug out some socks and a sweater to help Martha wrap up against the cold. It excited him to see her wearing his clothes. Soon, they were bounding through the deep snow toward the kids on the hill, laughing and talking as if they were part of the party.

For the next hour, they borrowed one sled after another and slid down the long hill, rolling off and then pulling the sled back up to do it again. Some kids showed up with a truck-tire inner tube. Another group brought a large piece of cardboard on which five or six kids gathered and went down the hill till it was soggy and began to break apart. Later in the afternoon, someone built a bonfire, and Chandler brought a couple logs down from his apartment as an offering to the fire. For now, thoughts of anything other than the moment were lost, and Flossie and Chandler became just two more children enjoying the first full snow of the winter sea-son.

When they returned to the apartment, Chandler was relieved to find no messages on the recorder. He restarted the fire while she shed her wet clothes and put his bathrobe on again. This time, they had hot chocolate while huddling in front of the fireplace.

"I guess we'll be closed tonight," she muttered. "Would you like a private show?"

"No, that's not what I want from you."

"What do you want?"

"I want you to...I want you to be happy. I want only good things for you." He hesitated, then added, "I want you to never go back to the Sunset again. You're too good for that."

She smiled softly and walked to the window.

"At the church," she said, "that Sunday I saw you. I wanted—"

"Wait a minute," Chandler said, astonished. "That was you in church last week, wasn't it? You came in for the service but left before it was finished. That was you, I can see it now."

Flossie nodded. "Yeah, that was me. I wanted to go to see if there was any feeling left. Somebody called that morning and told me Jaco was taken care of, that Flynn was dead, and that I would begin receiving more money because of it. It scared me. I wanted Jaco and that other son of a bitch hurt, but I didn't really want them killed. It was just something I said to feel better.

I didn't know what to do. So I did what I'd done all my life when I was in trouble: I went to church. And there you were. I knew who you were, and you were about to figure out who I was. That's why I left. I thought you were like all those other men—like Irv Rafferty, your damn boss. They go to strip joints on Saturday night and show up at church on Sunday morning, as if it's all right. It occurred to me then that church was not really a special place at all, not if the likes of you and Rafferty went."

"I'm sorry." He set his cup down and stared into her face. "I was at church because I had to speak to a class, but I didn't recognize you then. Don't judge me or the church by the fact that you just happened to catch us together."

She shrugged and looked away. "It doesn't matter. I shouldn't have gone anyway. And I won't go again. Church just doesn't do it for me anymore." She walked to the window. "The snow's letting up. Maybe it'll melt and I can get out of your hair."

"I don't think you'll ever be out of my hair. I want you in my hair. Whatever happens, even if you disappear again, you'll never leave me. I'm afraid for you to leave now. I might never see you again. Then I'll never know the rest of the story. I mean, I want to know who arranged the beating of Jaco, but even if you never tell me, I want you to not go away. You're—you're…"

"If you're asking me who beat Jaco, I don't know, for sure. And I didn't know he was dead, until you told me. I don't know who killed Nick either. Could I find out?

Probably. But I don't want to. That's the mistake you made. Sometimes people just have to mind their own business."

Chandler reached out to bring her back. "Martha, let's hit the slopes again."

She turned away. "I've got to go."

She grabbed her coat and started for the door. He begged her to wait, at least until the streets were plowed. But she didn't stop. He started to run after her, but he knew force was not something to which she would respond. So he stood at the window and watched as she disappeared down the hill toward Midlothian Turnpike.

23

For the first time in his career, Irv Rafferty sat in his office and ignored a major snow storm. A few times, he left his office, waddled quickly through the crowded, snow-frenzied newsroom and disappeared in the front office. Each time, he returned carrying papers and closed his office door behind him. Although his absence was appreciated, it drew the attention of the reporters and producers who scrambled to cover every angle on the weather. In the past, snow storms were one of the few events that routinely brought Irv into the newsroom flux. But today, he merely waddled around and clutched stack after stack of papers to his chest.

At two o'clock, Chandler arrived and tossed his keys on his desk. Alicia caught his eye and immediately invited him back outside for a private chat.

"Just to give you a heads up," she said, once the door had clicked shut behind them. "There's something coming down concerning Brady. I don't know what it is, but Irv is acting real weird."

"I'm not surprised. How is Brady?"

"He's fine, as far as I know, but he hasn't come in. And Irv totally ignored me when I asked about him."

"That's promising. I'll avoid Irv unless he says something to me. And thanks for the advice, Alicia. I mean, if we're going to do this news thing again this week, it helps for you to...you know what I mean?"

"Yeah, I'm sorry." She smiled. "I wasn't very nice to you last week. Really, I don't know why I treated you that way."

"No problem. Maybe it was me. I was pretty excited about playing anchorman."

"And you played it well. I should have said something."

"Let's go to work," he said. "It's cold out here."

Chandler held the door open for Alicia and followed her into the newsroom. Before he'd gotten a chance to fill his coffee cup, Irv opened his door and called out to him.

"Chandler, I need to see you immediately." Then he paused and added, "You too, Alicia. I want to see both of you immediately."

Chandler set his coffee cup down and eyed Alicia. She shrugged, and they walked together into Irv's office. With a grimly blank face, Irv stood behind his desk and nodded for Chandler to close the door.

"As of today," he said, "Chandler is the new anchorman. You two will anchor the news together. Brady will not return to the anchor desk. Are there any questions?"

Chandler and Alicia looked at each other, stunned.

"That's fine with me," Alicia said, evenly. "But what's the line on Brady? What do we say when people ask what happened to him? Like...what *did* happen to him?"

Irv shrugged. "We have decided, based on extensive research and following consultation with Brady, that it is in the best interest of him and us that we terminate our agreement. Brady actually asked for the out. He said he had some private business ventures he wanted to pursue, and we decided if he wanted to leave, it was best to do it now. That would give us time to gear up for the February book with you and Chandler. That's all there is to it. If someone asks, just say he decided to pursue other career opportunities."

Alicia smiled. "That's good enough for me. Is there anything else?"

"No, not now. I need to talk to Chandler alone."

Alicia turned to Chandler and shook his hand. Chandler nodded and waited for her to shut the door. Irv gathered some papers on his desk and shoved them toward Chandler.

"Glance over these and sign them—here, here and here."

"Sure, Irv. But what am I signing?"

"It's a five-year contract," Irv said, not looking at him. "A hundred-thirty thousand the first year, ten-percent increase annually after that. Standard clauses, do your job, all that stuff, no outs, a year non-compete after the end of the last year. Don't say anything to Alicia—it's more than she makes, a hell of a lot more. If you let it out, then I'll have to raise her salary too, so keep your damn mouth shut. Sign it now, you've got forty-eight hours to cancel, if you don't like anything. But that's not an option. Just sign the damn thing and go anchor the news. Oh yeah—you might want to read the moral turpitude clause. It says, in legal terms, to keep your ass away from places like the Sunset."

Chandler scanned the document. Then he took the pen and signed his name on the first copy and initialed the other four. Irv walked to his copy machine and made copies for Chandler.

"Was I that good?"

"You did all right," Irv said. He handed Chandler the copies. "There's more to it than that, but I don't intend to discuss it. Just take the money, anchor the news and be happy. I think that covers everything. You can go to work now."

"Thanks, Irv."

Chandler walked to his desk, plopped into the seat and looked around at his new, ill-gotten kingdom. He knew that the sequence of events punctuated by bloody noses, broken faces, and dead bodies was connected to his sudden rise to the coveted anchor post. And he suspected there would be a price to pay. As he stood up with his coffee cup, his phone rang.

"Congratulations, Chandler. I just heard the news."

It was Derrick Dimby, the TV reporter for the *Richmond Times-Dispatch*.

"What are you talking about?"

"Your promotion, Chandler. I just heard."

For a moment, Chandler didn't speak. "How did you hear?"

"Oh come now—is it true or not?"

"Sorry, Derrick. Any announcement will have to come from Irv. Wait a second. I'll transfer you."

Chandler pushed the appropriate buttons and sent the call to Irv. Then someone tapped him on the shoulder, and Chandler turned to see Clyde, the call-in volunteer, smiling down at him.

"Congratulations, Chandler," he shouted. "I just heard the good news."

"Thanks, Clyde. I—"

Before he could finish his sentence, Irv burst into the newsroom and demanded everyone's attention.

"I have a brief announcement," he said. "As of today, Chandler Harris is the new anchorman, replacing Brady Soles. Chandler and Alicia will anchor the six and eleven o'clock news. Brady has resigned to pursue other interests. That's all. Now go back to work."

Irv stepped back his office and slammed the door. Chandler looked quickly around the room for someone who might look like they were not surprised. There was no such person. Chandler leaned to Alicia's desk.

"Correct me if I'm wrong," he said. "But didn't Clyde congratulate me *before* Irv made the announcement?

"I think that's what I heard."

"Who told him?"

"That's a very good question. I have no idea."

For a few minutes, Chandler shook hands with the

various staff members who crowded around his desk to extend congratulations. Then he walked down the hall to the studio and watched the 4 News call-in volunteers work the phones.

Suddenly, the obvious smacked Chandler in the face: Clyde! His conversation with Flossie had been an open conversation because anyone in the area couldn't help but hear him shouting—and he never kept secrets. Chandler walked toward the phone bank, studying the volunteers' faces. Clyde. Dorothy. Allison. Shawn. There was only one possibility.

As Chandler reached the end of the table, Shawn leaned back in his chair with a smirk on his face. It said everything. Chandler stopped in front of him.

"Congratulations," Shawn said. "I just heard about your promotion."

"Seems like everybody's heard about it. Some before I did. It's you, isn't it?"

Shawn smiled. "You know, Chandler, I've thought for some time that you would be a great anchorman, and now you are. And you know, you earned it the hard way. We're proud of you. And mark my word: we'll support you every step of the way."

Chandler leaned over the table and lowered his voice. "We need to talk."

"This is not a good time," Shawn said, still smiling. "What with the snow and all, and your new responsibilities as anchorman. Meet me at Buddy's at seven o'clock tonight. I'll tell you how everything works and how you will be a part of it."

"I'm not a part of anything."

"Correction, Chandler: you are our most prominent partner now. You have no choice. I'll see you at Buddy's. And Chandler, this meal's on you. Now go be an anchorman. I've got to get back on the phone and counsel your viewers."

Four hours later, after sleepwalking through his first appearance as Richmond's premier anchor, Chandler drove across the river and found Shawn waiting for him in a corner table at Buddy's.

"You looked good tonight," Shawn said. "Like the job was made for you."

Chandler said nothing as the waitress arrived and set a water glass down in front of him.

"I'll be right back," she said. "We're awfully busy tonight. People like to go out for some reason when the weather's bad."

Shawn smiled, complacent, watching her leave, and then he leaned across the table until his face was hardly a foot from Chandler's.

"Welcome aboard," he said.

Chandler shook his head. "Don't play games, Shawn. You and I are never going to be a part of anything together."

"But we are—I am a public servant like you, you know," he said. "Like you, I work hard for the down and out, the helpless of society. I am a friend to the friendless. I turn no one away. While you are on TV getting the glory—and now the money—I am in the trenches of 4 News, reaching out to help those in need." He picked up his water glass and drank it all in a single swig. Then he signaled for the waitress to bring him a fresh glass. "We're a team. Do you understand what I'm saying? Alicia is just another pretty face. I am your co-anchor."

"I am aware of the good work 4 News does," Chandler said. "It is very important to the community and to our station. How do we get from that to gunning down a police officer?"

"I did not gun down a police officer." Shawn smiled as the waitress set a fresh water glass down on the table. "Nor did I authorize it," he added, after she had walked away. "I would never do such a thing. But I have an idea who did."

"Your buddy, Langetta."

"No, it wasn't Langetta."

"Then who was it?"

"You, Chandler. According to my information, *you* shot Officer Burke."

"So you're the one who called the police and said I killed him. You are crazy."

"No, I don't think so. The evidence speaks for itself."

"No motive, no murder weapon, just an anonymous caller who said they saw me do it. Not much of a case, I'd say."

"You're overlooking something, I think."

"And what might that be?"

Shawn leaned even closer to Chandler's face and

whispered a response that straightened Chandler in his chair. "According to what I hear, your fingerprints are all over the gun that killed Burke."

"What the hell are you talking about?"

"According to what I hear, your right index print is on the trigger, your left prints are on the barrel, there are prints on the clip, and every bullet remaining in the clip has at least one of your prints on it. Why, it's almost as if you loved that gun to death. You do remember that time you threatened to shoot our dear friend in Baltimore, don't you, Chandler?"

"You son of a bitch!"

"Hey, wait a minute. I'm your friend. I could have told the police about that gun—but I didn't, did I?"

"Langetta called you and told you I was stalking him," Chandler said, thinking out loud. "You, being the bastard you are, set me up at the Love Nest. How did you know I wouldn't pull the trigger and blow Langetta's ugly head off his shoulders?"

Before Shawn could answer, the waitress returned and asked them if they wanted any drinks. Chandler shook his head and said he'd stick with water. Shawn ordered a Diet Coke.

"I assured him you wouldn't do that," Shawn said, after the waitress left. "And I was right. You're not a killer, Chandler. You're an anchorman."

"And you're a cop killer planning to pin it on me, if I don't cooperate."

Shawn shrugged. "The killing of Officer Burke was an unfortunate mistake. I guess Josie had a tail light out or something, and he did the only thing he could do. He pulled the trigger and ran for his life. Burke would have nailed him on the Jaco thing for sure."

"How?"

Shawn leaned back in his seat and sighed. "These things are so tiresome, aren't they?"

Chandler said nothing, waiting.

"Langetta used to live in Richmond," Shawn finally said. "He was a cop. And he and Burke knew each other."

"You're lying!"

"Nope. He was one of Richmond's finest."

"What happened?"

"I forgot to give you gentlemen menus," the waitress called out, flustered. She laid menus down on the table and handed a Diet Coke to Shawn. "I'm sorry."

"No problem," Shawn said. "Take your time. We're in no hurry." He waited for her to cross the room. "Langetta couldn't separate his police life from his sex life. Like you, he spent too much time at the Sunset. Performing, if you will. Burke wasn't a great loss, though. He was a bad cop."

"That's not what I heard. I heard he was a good cop."

"Don't be fooled by the uniform," Shawn said, eyeing the room. "In most ways, Burke was no better than Josie, Nick, Jaco...or the others. Don't take his demise too seriously."

"The others?"

"I've been a public servant a long time."

"Flossie was getting money before Jaco was beaten.

How come?"

"I dogged him."

"Meaning?"

Shawn sipped his Coke. "That expensive dog that he has, nice dog. There used to be two of them. When Jaco refused to pay for his crime...Well, one of his dogs reminded him that we were serious."

"You killed his damn dog?"

"Saw it in a movie once. A real effective way of doing business. People are funny about their animals."

"So, if it works so well, why was Jaco beaten?"

"He stopped payments. Must have felt lucky. So we had to have Josie come to town."

"You keep saying 'we'."

"Yes, I do, don't I?"

There's someone else in this sorry business with you, isn't there?"

"You."

"That's not what I mean."

"Yes, as a matter of fact, there is. How do you think I found Josie?"

"From somebody familiar with his background, I imagine. Someone who knew he'd kill for a buck."

"Good guess." Shawn sipped his Coke and spilled a little of it on the table. "Josie's well-known in certain circles."

"Like the Sunset. I guess you hang out there too."

Shawn shook his head angrily. "Never been in the place."

"Why not? It's a nest of evil—I'd think you would

live there."

"Your problem, Chandler, is that you've got a distorted understanding of evil. But I'm going to help you work through it. I will teach you good from evil."

"Just like God."

"That's enough. You'll see the light in time. You have no choice. And in case you ever have the stupid idea of causing me a problem, remember the gun. And remember: I'm not working alone."

"You could be making that up."

"Could be."

"I'll have to wonder about that, right?"

"You'll never know."

"Irv Rafferty. You own him too."

"You could say that. We're friends."

"You've got something on him."

"Maybe."

"What?"

"You don't need to know."

"You only tell me what I need to know?"

"For the moment."

"Why did you decide to make me an anchorman?"

"You left me no choice."

"Meaning?"

"Meaning, you got a plate number and traced it to Langetta—which in your case would be easy to do."

"What do you mean?"

"Excuse me, Chandler, but didn't you introduce me to your wife two years ago at an office party?"

"You son of a bitch." Chandler felt like jumping

across the table and strangling the little man until he stopped grinning. "Leave Sarah out of this. She had no idea why I wanted that plate."

"Maybe."

"Damn it, leave her alone. She doesn't know anything."

"I'd like to believe that," Shawn said, expansively. "But remember: if you mess with me, I'll have to take care of business."

"Yeah, you take care of business, but listen to this, jerk. If anything happens to Sarah, I will personally kill you."

"Don't worry, Chandler. Sarah is fine, as long as you do what you have to do."

"Which is what?"

"For the moment, just pay the agency fee."

"Why am I not surprised? How much?"

"Five hundred dollars every two weeks, every pay check."

"And what, may I ask, do you do with the agency fee?"

"Expenses," Shawn said. "It goes for things like paying Flossie until the real money comes through. It pays Josie. It helps me out a little too, but mainly it reminds you every two weeks that you are a full partner in this worthy enterprise. The good news is that when we are able to build the operation to where I intend it to be, we will be able to eliminate your payments or at least reduce them significantly. It all depends on how cooperative you are."

"I assume I have no choice?"

"I don't know of any."

"Did I say you are a son of a bitch?"

"Yeah, I think you mentioned it a time or two. It would be nice if you didn't do that anymore. I'm getting tired of it."

"What else do I have to do?"

"I'll let you know. But don't worry. I won't do anything that would jeopardize your status as a successful anchorman."

"You need me. How touching."

"That makes us a team, Chandler: we need each other. As I said, we are co-anchors. Now let's order. The prime rib here is wonderful."

"You have prime rib," Chandler said, standing up. He threw a twenty-dollar bill on the table. "I'm out of here."

Shawn leaned back and smiled. "See you on TV."

24

Irv Rafferty sat staring at a cheap print of a beach scene on his wall when Chandler burst in and leaned menacingly over his News Director's desk.

"Okay, Irv, cut the crap. There's more to this than you told me, and I have a right to know."

"What the hell are you talking about?"

"Brady, me, you...God knows who else. The Sunset, for Pete's sake."

Irv shook his head and spun his chair away from Chandler. "I've already told you everything you need to know. Now get out of my face."

"If you don't tell me, I know someone who will," Chandler said.

He turned to leave, but Irv stopped him.

"I warned you about the Sunset," Irv said. "I could fire you tonight, if I find out you went there. And I don't care who would try to stop me."

"Well," Chandler said, opening the door. "When I find out who controls you, I'll mention you're tugging at the leash."

Chandler stormed out of Irv's office and sat fuming at his desk. A minute later, Irv burst out of his office and left the building without saying a word to anyone. An hour later, Chandler anchored the evening news as if it were the last broadcast on earth. Then, without looking back, he walked out of the station and drove recklessly to the Sunset.

He parked a couple blocks away from the parking lot and sat in his car for over an hour and watched. Shortly before closing time, he climbed out and navigated the snow-covered sidewalk to the Sunset.

"Flossie's not here tonight," Mary Anne said, as soon as he walked in.

"I want to talk to you. I'm a full member in this thing now, and I deserve to know what's going on."

"That could get us both killed."

"I could do that without your help."

Mary Anne smiled bitterly. "Okay, Chandler. Ask your questions."

They walked through the Sunset twilight and sat in a remote corner. Two girls wriggled on the bar while a handful of men idly watched and drank the last of their beer. Chandler set his elbows on the table but pulled them back when they stuck to the dried and sticky beer on the fake wood top.

Mary Anne lit a cigarette and raised an eyebrow. "Well?"

"I still can't figure out why Nick was beaten to death, and I have to know."

"Because he was a bad person."

"Come on, Mary Anne."

"Because he owed money and wouldn't pay it."

"Did he owe money to somebody at the TV station?"

"I don't know."

"You're not helping me, Mary Anne."

"Look, I told you he was a bad person. Bad people get beat up from time to time, and nobody cares."

Chandler shifted in his chair impatiently. "You told me he messed with the girls, he gambled, he abused people, he didn't pay his debts. You told me he'd been in trouble with the police. But there's got to be something more, something specific that might tie him to the television station...anything that would make that connection. Please, Mary Anne. I won't quit until I know. I'll be here every night until I know. If I have to, I'll make trouble for you. I don't want to, but I can, and I will. I have some new friends you might not care for."

She glared at him for a moment, drew on her cigarette and then glared again. "It might be Irv."

"Might be Irv what?"

"Nick made several feeble attempts at blackmail. When someone of prominence came in, like yourself, Nick would give them free drinks, make jokes and try to get them to play with the girls. Then he would go back there"—she motioned to the mirror behind the bar—"and take pictures."

"He took pictures of Irv fooling around?"

"It was worse than that."

"How so?"

She rose from the table and nodded for him to follow.

They walked into the office. She closed and locked the door and withdrew some papers from a file cabinet. She shuffled through routine invoices and handed Chandler a contact sheet. Not knowing what to expect, he held it up to the light. And saw a picture of Irv Rafferty, apparently sexually involved with someone. It was a tiny proof, but he could clearly make out Irv's face. He happened to be looking directly toward the two-way mirror with a look of intense excitement.

Mary Anne handed him a photographer's eyepiece. "Look closer."

Chandler held the eyepiece over the sheet and squinted at it.

"Damn! I don't believe it." He looked at Mary Anne, amazed. "Who is this?"

"I don't know," she said, shrugging. "Some guy. He never said what his name was. It's not a great picture. No one would ever notice it without magnification. That's the reason I keep the contact sheet. If anyone ever stumbled on it, they wouldn't see anything. But I know. I was here that night."

Suddenly, Chandler remembered the night Flossie crossed the room topless and shared a table with him. What if there were pictures of them together?

"Are there any pictures of me in here?"

Mary Anne laughed. "Relax, Chandler. There are a lot more pictures, but none of you. When Nick died, I put away the camera. If anyone ever comes in here, like with a search warrant, they can take that camera and find Nick's fingerprints all over it. You've got a lot of things to worry about, but I'm not one of them."

Chandler held up the contact sheet. "Can I have this?"

"I can't do that. I need it for protection. If anyone ever accuses me of hitting Nick, I can show them why someone else had reason to kill him. Besides, what if Irv messes with me? I mean, he knows too much. He knows I knew about the camera and what Nick was doing with it. He also knows about a lot of other stuff that went on here, and he could make a lot of trouble. I don't want that. I own this place now, and no weirdo like Irv is going to cause me to lose it. As long as Irv suspects I might have pictures, he will treat me like royalty."

"Did Irv kill Nick?"

"I doubt it. He's not that sophisticated."

"Beating someone to death is sophisticated?"

"Sometimes."

"What does that mean?"

Mary Anne shifted her weight and looked away from Chandler. "It means Nick's last beating may not have been as simple as it seemed."

Chandler stared at her, waiting.

"Nick was a punching bag," she finally said. "People were always getting mad at him and taking a few swings when he wasn't looking. But I saw him the night he died, and he didn't look like he did before. Not so gory and bloody, if you know what I mean."

"What are you saying?"

Mary Anne hesitated, choosing her words carefully.

"I'm saying that if you're thinking Nick was beaten to death by a big guy with a pony tail, you're wrong. But it may have been done to look like that. And that's all I'm going to say."

Chandler studied her face and wondered what to do next. "How many people know they were caught on film here?"

Mary Anne laughed loudly, relieved that he wasn't going to press her. "There are other pictures, lots of bad stuff of other upstanding citizens. Nick spent a lot of time with his camera. Sometimes, after we closed, Nick's best customers hung around. That's when the ugly things happened. Nick would set people up, then get pictures of them and let them know about it a few days later. He'd do anything to anybody for a buck."

"Did Irv pay?"

"I think so."

"For God's sake, Mary Anne! Why didn't you tell me this before?"

"If I had, what would you have done? It wasn't any of your concern before. The only reason I'm telling you now is that you're involved in this up to your butt, and you threatened me. I know enough to understand violence, now that you have...what did you call them, 'friends'?"

"Irv must know you have these pictures. You're not free yet."

Mary Anne shook her head. "I don't think so. I don't think anyone knows there are copies, except you and me. Irv only suspects it. That makes us friends, doesn't it, Chandler?"

Chandler grimly nodded and followed her out of the office. She stopped by the bar.

"That's it, Chandler. I told you everything I could. If there is more to know, you find it yourself. It can't come from me. I've told you everything I know. Anything else is just speculation."

Chandler nodded. "Thanks. You're about the only person in this sordid scheme that I trust. I want to trust Flossie too, but she's still messed up, I think. Is she going to be okay?"

"I don't know. She told me about spending the night with you, how you talked and all. She said you were a good listener. She said she wanted to talk to you some more, but not yet. She'll let you know. Don't give up on her. She's a good kid. She's just, like you said, messed up."

"Got any other advice for me?"

"Yeah. Quit trying to control this thing. Take what's been given to you and stay away from any ideas of trying to be a hero. You might also want to stay away from Irv. He's strange. Nothing he'd do would surprise me. Watch him."

"I'll keep that in mind."

Chandler threw the door open and, despite himself, looked around the parking lot before stepping out and walking back to his car.

25

Friday morning, after a bacon-and-eggs breakfast, Chandler drove to the Richmond Police's detective division and asked for the file on Nick Flynn. At first, the clerk refused, but she wilted under a barrage of Freedom of Information threats which she didn't understand. It was a bluff, but it worked.

Chandler took the stack of papers and sat down in a chair by the window. He shuffled through various arrest reports and found Nick's autopsy photos. Mary Anne was right: he was messy but not bloody, and his face wasn't puffed up.

Chandler dropped the stack on the clerk's counter and drove four blocks to the medical examiner's office. Chandler had to sit outside the empty basement office and wait thirty minutes, and then Dr. Henry Fieldstein showed up with a stack of reports and photographs under his arm.

"Congratulations," Fieldstein said, holding his free hand out. "You're an awfully young man for the anchor seat, though, aren't you? Did the station send you down here to make sure you were a good liability?"

They laughed together while Fieldstein opened his

office and tossed the stack of reports and photos onto his desk.

"Bureaucracy," he mumbled. "What can I do for you, Chandler?"

"Nick Flynn, the guy from the Sunset Bar and Lounge. You went over him, I guess?"

"Yeah. He was a weird one. No surprise, I guess. He lived weird, and he died weird."

"I was told he was beaten to death."

"Nope. Who told you that?"

"Don't worry about it."

"Oh. Right. Confidential sources."

Chandler shrugged and smiled. "So what really happened, Doc?"

"He got stuck with an ice pick."

"An ice pick!"

"Yep. Looked to me like one of his honeys slipped an ice pick into his heart and he gave up the ghost."

"But he was beaten too?"

"Technically, yes. But he was already dead by then. She killed him, then she picked up a brick and beat his dead body in a rage. There were particles of masonry in his skin. Cinder block, actually."

"That's the reason there wasn't much blood, right? Because his heart had already stopped pumping when he was beaten?"

"You got it, pal."

"But why do you say *she* beat him? Why not *he*?"

"An ice pick is not a murder weapon men usually use. And I don't think a man would beat a dirty old man after he's dead. The ice pick was too quick for the killer—using the brick let them vent some more spleen, so to speak. I'm not officially a detective, but that's what I think."

"Anything else weird about Nick?"

"Not really. Except his arteries."

"His arteries?"

"Yeah. The guy was so clogged up he could have dropped dead at any time. He had already out-lived his body's capacity, in my opinion. Alternative lifestyles have their price."

"Thanks, Doc. You've been a great help."

"Anytime. Are you sure you don't want a physical while you're here?"

Chandler stood up and shook his head. "No thanks. I'll wait until my time."

Chandler left the morgue and drove slowly to the television station, musing over the new information. Beating a man to death was one thing; slipping an ice pick into his chest was another. Fieldstein was right: a woman might be more likely than a man to do that. He pulled up to the toll booth at the Boulevard Bridge and tossed a quarter into the bin. Who knows: maybe it was Mary Anne after all. Or even Flossie. He hated the thought. He accelerated over the bridge and watched the river flicker through the guard rails.

Traffic was lighter on the Turnpike than it had been in weeks, and he reached the station in less than ten minutes and parked in a spot next to the side door. Inside, he nodded at a few reporters and poured himself a cup of coffee. As he sipped at it and looked around the newsroom, he couldn't shake the thought that Flossie might be the one who killed Nick—though, he quickly told himself, he didn't believe that for a moment. She just couldn't do that, not Flossie, not Martha Carpenter. There had to be a better explanation, something that made sense but didn't hurt Martha. But what if it he found out otherwise? Would he be willing to turn her in?

Chandler sipped his coffee, pondering. Then, after crossing the room for a refill, he picked up his phone.

"Brenda," he said, after a moment. "How would you like to follow the trail to Bill Burke's murder?"

"Chandler, don't play with me. If you've got something, let me have it."

He hesitated, thinking of Flossie in the snow. "Brenda...did you know that Nick Flynn was stabbed with an ice pick, and that his murderer may have been a woman?"

"Who told you that?"

"Sources."

"What sources?"

"Forget that. Assume it's true. Does that cause you to have renewed interest?"

"Not necessarily. I haven't personally looked at his case. I told you, Flynn was not a high priority. But you say he was picked—what happened to the fact that his head was bashed in? Seems to me that would be sufficient."

"It would have been, but it happened *after* he was dead. Hey, check the report—the M.E.'s got it on his desk. I just left there."

"So that's where you got it. Fieldstein. You've got no right to that information, Chandler. Fieldstein could be in trouble."

"I suddenly deny it was Fieldstein. So what do you do now?"

"Okay, wise guy. Forget that. So Flynn was stabbed and beaten. How does that tell you who killed Officer Burke?"

"What it tells me is that someone wanted Nick's killing to look like something it wasn't. That someone knew how Jaco was hurt and wanted to make it look like the same person did Nick."

"So what's that got to do with Officer Burke?"

"Jaco's attacker killed Burke."

"Can you prove that?"

"Yes," Chandler said. "But not right now."

"Who was it, Chandler?"

"I can't tell you. You figure it out. You're the police."

"You seem to forget that from time to time."

"Talk to Mary Anne—she knows. Then put two and two together, and when you're convinced that the killings are connected, give me a call. And I'll not only give you the killer's name, I'll give you his address. And there's one more person involved in this. When you get that far, I'll give him to you as well. Trust me.

The Sunset Lounge

I know what I'm doing. But don't use my name in any way. There are people who would kill me without a second thought if they knew I'd talked to you. Fair enough?"

"Okay, Chandler. You've got a deal. If a single iota of your theory stacks up, I'll owe you an apology. But I'm doing this as much as a favor as anything else. I don't really think you've got anything."

"I've got what we need, Brenda. You make one move in the right direction, and I will supply you with additional information. Who knows — you might be in line to be the Chief of Police."

"I won't be holding my breath."

Chandler hung up the phone and took a long sip of coffee. Then, gathering up his courage, he stood up and strode into Irv's office.

"So how much is it costing you, this sham to keep the picture quiet?"

Irv's head shot up from a list of ratings. "Close the damn door."

Chandler reached behind him and swung the door shut.

Irv threw his reading glasses down on the desk and waddled around to Chandler's side. "Where did you see the picture?"

"It doesn't matter," Chandler said. "I saw it. You'd better talk to me, Irv. Maybe we can help each other."

Irv studied Chandler's face and shrugged. "It's no

big deal. I was at the Sunset, that son of a bitch pushed this babe in my lap and took a picture. Then he tried to sell it to me."

"Did you buy it?"

"Yeah, a couple of times. Every time Nick needed more cash, he'd sell me another copy."

"So you killed him."

"No, I just wanted to."

"So you hired someone to kill him."

"Get real, Chandler. The photo's no big deal. Even if it comes out, I can probably survive it. I wasn't doing anything with the girl, she was just in my lap."

"Girl?"

Irv froze.

"Listen, Irv. I told you: I've seen the picture. And the babe was no girl. The print is bad, but it's not that bad."

Irv turned pale and reached for a cigarette, then slammed his lighter on the desk when it didn't light. Chandler calmly picked it up and flipped it once to light Irv's cigarette. Irv drew on the cigarette twice and coughed. Then he walked back around the desk and sank in his chair, deflated.

"What do you want from me? I've given you all the money I can squeeze out of the budget. My ass is on the line, if this thing goes wrong."

"All I want is the truth," Chandler said. "Don't worry about me hurting you. Remember, I owe you. You made me an anchorman and gave me a hundred-thousand dollar raise. So tell me: how did you get caught on film at the Sunset playing with another man?"

"I was set up."

"By whom?"

"You know damn well by whom. Quit playing dumb."

"Shawn?"

"Of course. Shawn made me do it. Shawn's the one with the picture. He got it from Nick after he paid Nick to take it. He set me up, then threatened me with the picture until I gave in to save my reputation, my job and my family. That's all I wanted."

"So Nick gave you the picture?"

"Sure he did. Several times. Then Shawn showed me his copy. He'd had it all along. They were in business together."

"Why would Shawn want to set you up?"

Irv stubbed the cigarette out and lit another one. "Because he wanted to make sure I'd give Ragland an alibi."

For a moment, Chandler merely gawked. "Roger Ragland?"

Irv nodded. "The night his wife was killed, Ragland was with me at the Sunset. I didn't know it at the time, but I was his alibi. I didn't know about the hit on his wife, though. I had nothing to do with it. And I for damn sure didn't know about the camera."

"So Ragland hired Shawn to kill his wife?"

"Yes, sort of."

"What do you mean, 'sort of'?"

"Shawn told Ragland he wouldn't do it, but he did

know a hit man."

"And Ragland called in the hit man?"

"I think so."

"He didn't like his wife, I guess."

"She was the worst. She was doped out half the time, and the other half she was busy spending the good doctor's money on drugs. She was also, I am told, eager to do just about anything to get what she had to have. Dr. Ragland had no alternative except to get rid of her."

"He never heard of divorce, I guess."

"Yes, but he had also heard of alimony, and the last thing he was going to do was let her get her hands on the rest of his money."

Chandler sat down in the chair across from Irv and shook his head. "Why didn't it work?"

"Why didn't *what* work?"

"The alibi," Chandler said. "You were never called to testify. No one even knew about you."

"Ragland's lawyers were told in no uncertain terms that if I was called, I would deny being with him. That would have made Ragland look like a liar. So I was never called."

"But what about the photo? Didn't Shawn try to use it against you?"

Irv laughed bitterly. "Shawn's not the sort of guy you can trust with your life. Especially if you've given him all your money, and he has no more use for you. Just ask Ragland's headstone. Ragland was a liability, and Shawn decided the photo was worth more to him than Ragland's life was, I suppose."

The Sunset Lounge

"But you could have saved his life."

Irv set the cigarette on the edge of the ashtray. "Yes, in exchange for my own. It was a no-brainer. His life or mine. Shawn told me that Ragland had tried to hire him for the hit, so he was deserving of what he got. I tried to think of it that way."

"So your going with the live shot with Ragland on the day of the execution—that was like Pilot washing his hands."

Irv shrugged. "I couldn't just sit there and do nothing. I had to do something to clear my conscience."

"Did it help?"

"Not much."

"What's to keep me from telling all this to the police?"

"You have no reason to do that, and every reason not to, that's why."

Chandler weighed the answer and, overall, had to agree. "So what happens now?"

"Unless you are prepared to kill Shawn and hope that he's acting alone, nothing happens now. You anchor the damn news, I run the news department and life goes on."

Chandler watched the news director draw on his cigarette and twitch. "Irv, you've got to stop smoking cigarettes. They're going to kill you. I'm going to anchor the news now. You take care. Maybe Shawn will have a bad accident or something."

"Worse things have happened. Good luck, Chandler."

Chandler looked at the hapless news director. For the

first time in his life, he felt sorry for him.

26

Chandler walked back to his desk and logged onto his computer. After glancing over his shoulder, he typed a message to Shawn.

"I have a job for us. Do we do charity work?"

He printed the message out on the line printer and erased it from the computer. Then he sealed the note and left it in Shawn's mail box. On his way back, he noticed his pay check sitting in his own box. Back at his desk, he opened the envelope and gawked at the total: eighteen hundred dollars for one week of work. Even with the deduction for Shawn's operation, he was hundreds ahead of where he was before being forced into the anchor chair. Despite himself, he had to admit that the promotion had its good sides. As long as it didn't crumble around him before he was finished.

Chandler slipped the check into his pocket and drove to the bank. He deposited most of it but kept enough out to fill his vest pocket with fifty-dollar bills. After driving back to the station, he filled his coffee cup and pushed some paper around on his desk. Then he walked down the hall and checked his box. A plain white envelope waited for him. Chandler carried the envelope to the bathroom, and, after assuring himself that Woody wasn't sitting in the adjacent stall, he opened it.

"Yes," the note said, "we do charity work. All our work is for the good of the community. Money is collected only to cover overhead. What is the good deed you speak of?"

Chandler walked back to his desk and typed another note on his computer. "There's a guy at the World Mission Agency who owes Flossie. He was with Jaco when she was raped. His real name is Ralph Adkins. He is director of missionary placement. I'm not sure what form it will take, but for Flossie, I want justice."

As he had done before, Chandler printed it out and put it in Shawn's mail box, along with a stack of fifty-dollar bills—his agency fee, as Shawn had called it. For the rest of the day, he made excuses to check his mail box, but there was no response from Shawn.

He spent the weekend waiting, trying to read, watching television, avoiding the Sunset. It dragged by. He imagined Martha, dancing on the bar. He hated the thought. He would save her, even if it cost him his own soul.

Shawn's response was in the mail box Monday morning: "I will talk to him."

For the next week, neither Shawn nor Chandler left messages in the boxes. Chandler avoided the Sunset, Irv avoided Chandler, and the new routine as anchorman settled in. Everybody went about his business.

Then on Friday afternoon, when Chandler went to retrieve his pay check from his office mail box and leave a stack of fifty-dollar bills for Shawn, he found Shawn's response: "Offer rejected. Adkins denies cooperation. *You* contact Baltimore and use key words, 'This is R-I-C.' He will do what you say."

Damn, Chandler thought. *He wants me to order the hit!*

He insisted in a return note that Shawn make the call, but Shawn rejected it without hesitation. Chandler knew he had no other choice, so he sat down and typed out another message: "Do I call or write?"

"Write," Shawn responded, late in the afternoon. "From the computer. Calls can be recorded, and this one had better not be. Besides, he might recognize your voice. I can call, you cannot. He knows you, remember. Seal the letter with tap water, salvia leaves DNA. Give him everything he needs to know, but nothing more. Include five hundred now, fifteen hundred later. No checks, of course. Use your own money, we will replenish it later. That's the way it works sometimes. Seed money, you know."

Chandler was relieved that he wouldn't have to talk to Langetta on the phone. He also liked the fact that Langetta would not know who sent the letter. So after driving to the bank and cashing his check, he sat down in front of his computer and composed a note, though it was more than what he had discussed with Shawn.

"Two hits," he wrote. "One is light—injuries, but nothing more. The other—more. Go all the way." He gave the names and addresses of the victims. Then he printed the note out and sealed it and a thousand dollars in an envelope with tap water and applied the stamp. On the way home, he wiped the envelope clean and dropped it in a drive-through mail box.

Then he waited.

The difference between accepting something that has been done and anticipating its happening began to weigh on him. He knew that a man was going to be beaten, perhaps badly, because of him. And another man would die, if everything went well. The death he could accept; it was, after all, the only way to stop the nightmare he found himself inside. But he worried about Adkins. What if Adkins died too? Then he would be a murderer twice-over. The thought scared him badly.

When he'd made the arrangements, he was thinking of what happened to Brady, imagining someone bashing Adkins in the mouth for ruining Flossie's life. That seemed just. But now he began thinking of Nick and Burke. How things could get out of control before you realized it. He stood up and paced the length of his apartment, cursing the day he'd thought so little of investigating an assault in River Heights. Still, he had more than he had imagined. Money, fame—and he was an anchorman. He wanted two things more: Flossie and the elimination of the circumstances that brought him to her.

He sat down on the bed and picked up the phone. He dialed Information and waited.

"Baltimore," he said, when the operator answered. "Business listing. I'd like the number of the Love Nest."

He memorized the number the operator gave him and immediately dialed it. Someone picked up on the fourth ring, and Chandler asked for Josie. He could hear the phone hit the bar counter with a sharp click, and in the background, the same band was playing—or one nearly as bad. A minute later, the phone was picked up again, and the sultry voice that Chandler had hoped never to hear again answered.

"This is Josie."

Chandler hesitated, then grabbed a handkerchief to muffle his voice. He hoped with the background noise in the Love Nest and his own muffled voice, Langetta would accept his being Shawn.

"The order from R-I-C," he mumbled. "You've got two jobs. Do the first one light—as usual, but not bad. Have your fun with the other one. The first one, only a little bit, got it?"

There was a pause on the other end of the phone, as if Langetta were trying to decide if the call was real.

"Okay, honey," Langetta finally said. "Just a little bit."

Chandler hung up the phone. The conversation had lasted less than thirty seconds. For a moment, he was relieved. Then he panicked: *he had called the Love Nest long-distance from his own phone.*

He fell back on the bed and waited for the sirens to come. He was sweating, and he decided that, barring imminent arrest, he needed a drink. He stood up after a minute and walked to the kitchen.

"I'm not cut out for this work," he told himself, reaching for a beer.

27

The next night, he came out of the studio after the late news and found his phone ringing. It was Brenda Montgomery.

"I've got something for you," she said. "Are you sitting down?"

"Go ahead."

"One of your 4 News volunteers has been hurt. Shawn—you know the funny little guy who sits over on the end. He's at MCV. Somebody beat the crap out of him."

"Is he hurt badly?"

"I think so," she said. "He may not make it. There's no brain activity. He was picked up in his own front yard. Sap glove again. Like Jaco. Except this time, the guy apparently went too far. His head's bashed in. They're keeping him alive with tubes, so the family can prepare for the disconnect. Just thought you'd like to know."

"Thanks, Brenda," Chandler said, his face feeling warm. "I'll run by the hospital and see how he is. Any witnesses?"

"None that we can find. You don't sound surprised,

Chandler. Is there something wrong?"

"No, nothing. I've just learned to accept things like this. It's part of the newsman thing, I guess."

"You'll let me know if you have any ideas who might have ordered the hit on Shawn, won't you?"

"Of course, Brenda. I've always talked to you. And thanks for the tip. Sooner or later, we'll find out who's doing this. It's a damn shame."

Two hours later, sirens could be heard as Chandler drove slowly to his apartment. For once, he didn't care what story they might offer. He had accomplished what only a few days earlier had seemed impossible: the elimination of a renegade 4 News star volunteer. Tonight, he would sleep soundly.

Langetta would not know for at least a few days who his victim had been. Then Chandler would have to settle his last score. The thought didn't bother him, surprisingly. He knew a dark alley in Baltimore where a gun shot in the early morning hours would attract little attention. He would have to do it himself. There was no one left to hire. It was the only way to end the killing, including the likelihood of his own.

He parked in front of his apartment and climbed the steps upstairs. The air smelled musty, but he didn't bother with the fan. Instead, he simply walked into the bedroom and lay on the bed, staring at the ceiling. Streams of pink-tinged light from the street lamps slipped through the blinds and bounced playfully on the wall beside him. He wondered who he was now, if he were in fact the different person he seemed to be. The very idea of initiating violence did not seem as strange as it once had. Or as bad, given a good cause.

He started to drift asleep but his eyes opened immediately when he heard what sounded like a key in the door. Lying perfectly still, he could see the shadow of a figure move slowly into the apartment, through the living room and toward his bedroom. It was coming for him. Slowly, he slipped from the covers to the floor, reaching back to tuck the pillows under the quilt as if he were still lying there, unaware. As he cowered beside the dresser, the intruder stepped into the doorway, raised a pistol to eye level and fired three muffled shots into his bed. Acrid smoke filled the room. The intruder then walked closer to the bed and bent over to make sure the work was done.

With courage he never imagined, Chandler sprang up and flung himself against the back of the intruder. The intruder immediately collapsed against the wall. Without looking back, Chandler bolted for the door. Before he'd taken three strides, two more shots followed him up the hall. Chandler stumbled and fell. He turned back to the bedroom in time to see the intruder raise his gun and aim it at Chandler. There was no chance of escape.

Chandler cringed, waiting. Then, before the intruder could shoot, the apartment's front door swung wide open and someone yelled, "Stay down!" Obediently, Chandler lay flat and watched the second figure reach over him and fire four shots toward the bedroom. Then there was silence, and a putrid cloud of black smoke rose through the beams of street light.

For a moment, Chandler lay still. Then the apartment lights came on, and he looked up to see Patrolman Glen Robinson standing over him with his gun drawn. He motioned for Chandler to stay down while he moved cautiously down the hall. Chandler watched as Robinson held his gun on the person crumpled on the floor. Robinson felt for the switch and turned on the bedroom light. He bent down to check for a pulse. Then he put his gun away and walked slowly back to Chandler.

"Go ahead, have a look," said Robinson. "Then come back and we'll have a little chat."

Chandler walked to the bedroom, where he leaned against the wall for support and looked into the lifeless eyes of Captain Brenda Montgomery.

"I don't believe this," he said, shaking his head as he continued to watch a pool of blood seep from under Montgomery's body. "I do not believe this."

He retreated to the couch in the living room and sat gazing straight ahead. The flashing lights of the ambulance and patrol cars parked outside were lighting up the walls in flashes of red and blue, and even if the widow downstairs survived the shock of the sudden attention, Chandler knew he'd lost a viewer.

"How did you know?"

"You told me," Robinson said.

He waited in silence until the stretcher bearing Brenda's body was wheeled out of the living room. Chandler looked away and concentrated on the sound of a squeaky wheel rolling across the carpet.

"That Saturday morning," Robinson said, when they were alone again. "You and I were on a common mission. I watched you dig around on the Jaco case and come up dry. I dug around on it and kept being told to forget it—just like she told you to forget it. The more she pushed me away, the more I watched her. Everything has its reason."

"But why Brenda? I thought it was all Shawn."

"He was part of it. But I was out there many times for those 4 News things, and Shawn and Brenda spent an unnatural bit of attention on each other. That's when I started to snoop around at the department, and I noticed things. Like the Captain's lifestyle. She lived far beyond her means. And I found out more about her relationship with the late Officer Burke. Like him, she was out to impose justice her own way. It's called taking the law into your own hands. Not exactly a new idea."

"Dumb question," Chandler said, sipping the coffee Robinson had made while waiting for things to calm down. "How come everybody seems to have a key to my apartment?"

Robinson smiled. "We're all creatures of habit. Every day at work, you walk in and toss your keys and your date book on your desk. I've seen you do it myself.

And every day a hundred people walk by your desk, 4 News volunteers included. Anyone could borrow your keys for fifteen minutes and run across the street to the hardware store for a copy."

"I guess I'll change my locks."

"No need for that, you're safe now."

"Not quite," Chandler said. "There's a guy in Baltimore who doesn't like me very much."

"Who?"

Chandler hesitated and then decided to tell him. He had saved his life, after all. "His name's Joe Langetta."

Robinson smiled again. "I wouldn't worry about him."

"You would, if you knew him."

"I do know him. Or did."

"Did?"

"Yeah. Langetta's lying on a slab at the morgue. Brenda killed him tonight."

Chandler almost dropped his cup of coffee. "Are you serious?"

"Quite serious. And we'd better get that coffee stain up before it sets." He went into the kitchen and came back out with a dish cloth, which he tossed under Chandler's knees. "You might want to put your foot on that. My wife would kill me if I spilled coffee at home. Now what was I saying? Oh. Brenda and Langetta. She pulled him over on I-95 just inside the city limits and shot his brains out. She said he pulled a gun on her, and he did have a gun on him. But he never drew it. He worked for her, and he had no reason to suspect she was about to kill him. I'd like to have seen the expression on his face."

"Why did she kill him, and why did she try to kill me?"

Robinson shrugged. "You scared her. Shawn thought you could be bought. Brenda couldn't take that chance. She apparently hired Langetta to kill Shawn. Then she followed him from the crime scene and pulled him."

Chandler's thoughts caught up with him. Robinson had figured everything out, except for who killed Shawn. But it was best left alone.

"She wanted Shawn killed?"

"I guess so," Robinson said. "Langetta did it, didn't he? There's nobody else who could have arranged it, and she had her reasons. She probably agreed to help Langetta, as usual. I think he checked with her every time he came to town to make sure she would keep the cops clear of his target."

"So you were on to this long before I was?"

"I was. I had been watching her for a long time, and I had been watching your volunteer buddy. Brenda knew everything Shawn did. She knew he had sucked you in, and she didn't like it. What she didn't know was whether you knew about her. If you didn't, Shawn might decide to tell you, and then she faced a blackmail risk—at best. And that's why she couldn't take the chance."

"So who killed Nick Flynn? Mary Anne?"

"Not a chance. She wouldn't set herself up like that."

"But Nick did."

"Nick was in it up to his ass. Unfortunately for Nick, his ass was located between his ears. That's about it, I guess. Why don't you run on over to the Day's Inn and catch a good night's sleep? I need to get my crew in here to clean up your apartment."

"You saved my life."

"It's no big deal. When I can, I save a life. It doesn't matter if it is an anchorman. A life's a life. And take your key. I'll use Brenda's when we lock up."

Chandler grabbed a jacket and started out.

"Hey, Chandler," Robinson said.

"Yeah?"

"Brenda did Nick."

Chandler stopped and turned around. "How?"

"She walked calmly up to him in the parking lot and slipped an ice pick into his chest. Think about it. Langetta hits Jaco, then goes crazy and shoots Burke. Brenda panics and begins eliminating weak links in her ring of thugs. Nick was famous as a weak link, easily bought and prone to turn on his friends, like Irv. She did it that night because she knew it would get no attention in the wake of a cop killing."

"And she tried to make it look like a beating."

"Right. After he was down, she beat his face in a bit."

"How do you know all this?"

"Goodnight, Chandler. Sleep well."

"Lieutenant. Wait a minute. This is epiphany time."

"I suppose."

"Jaco had a pick in his chest, just like Nick. That

explains how she just happened to be at the hospital when he died. But how did she know I was on my way? How did she set me up?"

Robinson just stood there, as if waiting for Chandler to reach his own conclusion. Chandler squinted his eyes and glared at Robinson.

"You. You were tailing me. That's how you figured all this out. Brenda had you tailing me. You told her I was headed to MCV. You knew, didn't you, Lieutenant? You knew when Jaco died that Brenda was Nick's killer because she did it the same way. That's when you knew, when Jaco was killed. All of a sudden, you knew that your boss, Brenda Montgomery, was a murderer. Right?"

Robinson contorted his face. "As I said, Chandler, sleep well."

"Wait! My car. Why did they blow up my damn car?"

"That was a mistake, Chandler. Bad timing."

"Bad timing?"

"Yeah. You weren't in it."

The two men continued to look at each other for a moment. Then Chandler walked slowly into the night.

28

Two days later, an emergency meeting of the board of directors and administration was called at the World Mission Agency. Eighteen of the highest ranking officials were seated around the long table in the board room when Ralph Adkins walked in. His face was red and puffy with black splotches across his right cheek, and he limped slightly as he approached the head of the table. George Payne jumped from his chair and rushed to Adkins.

"Ralph—what happened?"

Adkins raised his hand and motioned for Payne to take his seat. Then Adkins pulled from his vest a piece of paper and began to read in a quivering voice. He confessed fully to the rape and his denial of it. He further admitted that it was his intention to remain silent about the weekend in Atlanta and deny it if it ever came up again, as it had when he encountered Martha Carpenter at the World Mission Agency.

Adkins concluded by offering his resignation. Then he turned and walked away from the stunned board of directors. For several long seconds, no one spoke. Then the chairman of the board rose and began to pray.

The following day, the board sent to the *Times-Dispatch* a news release that read:

"Ralph Adkins, Director of Missionary Placement for the Richmond-based World Mission Agency, resigned as of January 16. Adkins will be replaced by Harvey Parker, currently serving as Field Coordinator for Missionary Services."

The press release was sufficient for a brief mention in the religious section of the paper.

Two days later, three middle-aged men in polyester blend shirts, ties and suits walked timidly into the Sunset Lounge and sat in a corner. They ordered three Cokes and then asked to speak to Martha Carpenter. The waitress said there was no such person there, but Mary Anne overheard the conversation. After a brief exchange with the strange visitors, Mary Anne called Flossie over from the bar. At first, Flossie refused to join them. But Mary Anne insisted, and finally she led Flossie to the table and left her with the three men.

Flossie, naked except for a G-sting, sat down and immediately asked her visitors for a cigarette. None of them had one. They stared awkwardly at their Cokes.

"I'm Jerry Garner," one of the men finally said, while the others looked away. He was careful to look directly into Flossie's eyes and not let his attention seem to wander. "These gentlemen and I are representatives from the World Mission Agency."

Flossie jumped to her feet and ran back to the bar.

While the other men sat stiffly, Garner went after her, begging her to hear them out. Flossie turned back to them, glaring, and finally she walked back and sat down.

While the others tried to find something safe to look at, Garner explained that the World Mission Agency was in mourning about the events that had been laid to it. As he spoke, he handed Flossie an envelope.

"While this can in no way compensate for the evil that has been done to you," he said, "it is a token of our regret for your pain and suffering caused by Ralph Adkins."

Flossie opened the envelope and pulled out a check for fifty-thousand dollars. "I don't want your apologies or your money," she said. "I want to be left alone."

She threw the check on the table and rose to leave.

"Please," Garner said. "We're trying to do the right thing, Ms. Carpenter."

Flossie turned away, staring at the bar. There was brief silence. Then tears began to roll down her cheeks, and she turned and confronted the men.

"Why don't you give me what I really want, what I lived my life for? Why don't you make me a missionary? I mean, you believe in forgiveness, don't you? That's what you preach. If what you say you believe is true, then I can be whiter than snow, can't I? But instead, you toss me thirty pieces of silver. You're no better than the thug who caused you to come here."

Garner followed her to the bar and touched her shoulder.

The Sunset Lounge

"I believe in everything I have lived my life for," he said, in a low, steady voice. "There was a Judas among us, and he has injured us all. He has brought shame on God, the World Mission Agency and himself."

He reached into his pocket and handed Flossie a handkerchief.

"I want you to leave this place tonight," he said. "Get your clothes and walk out and never look back. I want you to come to the Agency and show that you mean what you say. Forgive us. Forgive Ralph Adkins. We want you very badly. We've prepared a place for you at the New Kent Training Center. We want you, Martha. God needs you. Please come home."

Flossie was shaken. Tears swelled up in her eyes again, and she began to tremble. She looked down at her naked body and slowly drew her arms across her bare chest. Garner shed his suit coat and handed it to her.

"No," she shouted.

She threw the coat aside and ran back to the bar. She jumped up on the bar and began to dance wildly, gyrating and pushing her body toward patrons who eagerly reached out to stick dollar bills in her G-string.

With his head bowed, Garner walked back to the table and nodded for the other two men to follow him out. At the door, they stopped briefly to glance back at what had almost been a miraculous conversion.

Then they went out.

Flossie, watching them leave, stopped dancing, stood erect on the bar and screamed. The music stopped.

Everyone set their drinks down and watched. For a moment, the atmosphere was fearful. The three-piece band held their instruments and looked in amazement as Flossie jumped from the bar and ran out the door to Garner, who was still lingering outside with his coat in his hand.

"Take me," she said.

He draped the coat around Martha as Mary Anne rushed out after her.

"My God," she said. "Are you all right?"

Martha smiled sheepishly and hugged her. "I'm leaving now," she said. "It's time for Flossie to go."

Then she and the three dowdy men from the World Mission Agency walked quickly into the darkness. Mary Anne leaned against the door and allowed one tear to roll from her cloudy eyes, through the makeup and down her cheek.

Then she rubbed it dry and went back to work.

Epilogue

On March twenty-third, a late winter storm covered Richmond with a blanket of wet snow. Late that night, the city was virtually paralyzed as the snow accumulated to nearly sixteen inches in depth. It was partially because of the storm that firefighters were late in responding to a multi-alarm fire on the Southside which leveled the Sunset Bar and Lounge. The building and everything in it were destroyed. Fortunately, because of the weather, the Sunset had closed earlier in the evening, and no one was present when the fire started. There were no injuries.

Fire investigators suspected arson, but it was never proved. Mary Anne, who had been advised earlier to make sure she had proper insurance coverage, collected the money and moved away. No one in Richmond ever saw her again.

Patrolman Robinson, in part because of his outstanding work in breaking up a police corruption ring, was promoted to Captain of Detectives, a position left vacant by the death of Brenda Montgomery.

The February news ratings of WRT-TV revealed in late March that Channel 4 was far ahead of the other two competing stations. Irv Rafferty, determined to cash in on his success, resigned as news director and started his own consulting firm.

Chandler Harris signed a new multi-year contract with an escape clause, stipulating that while he could not work for another television station in Virginia, he could leave with sixty days' notice, if offered a position in a major city or with one of the major television networks.

Before signing the contract, Chandler convinced the station to underwrite a minimum of one foreign trip each year to allow him to boost his reputation as a serious reporter and at the same time provide a break from the sometimes boring routine of anchoring the evening news.

In early June, following Sarah's wedding to Bill, Chandler made a connecting flight at Baltimore-Washington International Airport for Nairobi, Kenya, where he would prepare a series of reports on a missionary journeyman from Richmond.

It was a legitimate news story for which he would later receive a national press award. For the first time, the World Mission Agency had assigned a former topless dancer to a mission field at its main headquarters in East Africa.